DEC 1 7 2019

D0765352

DRAGULA

DRAGULA

Ma'am Stoker

Sophie Wilson
in consultation with Andrew Heron

First published in Great Britain in 2018 by Trapeze,
an imprint of The Orion Publishing Group Ltd
Carmelite House, 50 Victoria Embankment,
London EC4Y 0DZ

An Hachette UK company

1 3 5 7 9 10 8 6 4 2

A CIP catalogue record for this book is
available from the British Library.

ISBN (Hardback): 978 1 4091 8110 1
ISBN (ebook): 978 1 4091 8111 8

Typeset by Born Group

Printed and bound in Great Britain by Clays Ltd, Elcograf S.p.A.

www.orionbooks.co.uk

For Emily
Brontë, you slay

Prologue

Gather round, children, of Houses far and wide,
For a tale of rivalry, sequins and one unholy bride.
My name is Ma'am Stoker and I'll be your host,
Prepare for a thriller tale, I don't mean to boast.
I'll serve two titans of the scene, united in hate.
(The costumes are cheap but the lip syncs are great.)
Our first lady Dragula needs no introduction,
Renowned for art-house, fangs and a strong sense of suction.
Her nemesis Van High Heelsing is Dam fine, it's true,
Fond of rubber, latex and a facial filler or two.
Are you ready for horrors, for blood on the runway?
For Dragula's daughters are ready to play . . .

YASSSSS KWEEN I hear you scream
But patience – we must first set our scene
With Jonathan Harker,
A most basic bitch
Travelling through Europe with barely a glitch,
Until he reaches Transylvania's border,
And things start to get somewhat disordered . . .

PART ONE

Chapter 1

Finally! thought Jonathan Harker, as he glimpsed a 'Welcome' sign to Tuckerweiner-von-Sea. It had been an arduous journey to the heart of Transylvania, and he was delighted to arrive at the village where he would spend the night before journeying on to Castle Dragula the following day.

Tuckerweiner-von-Sea was a strange place, mused Jonathan, noting the chipped mirrorballs hanging haphazardly from a signpost. It gave the impression of having once been a bustling village that had now faded from its past glory. Several shops had closed down, leaving only their signage – a manicurist, two hairdressers, a plus-size lady's shoe shop, a fabric stall, a Party City . . . Jonathan supposed this must have been some kind of spa town back in the day.

He also spied various tattered posters as the horse and cart trundled through the streets. He managed to make out the lettering on one, which advertised a show by Hairy Shelley – a remarkable-looking woman who also had a luxuriant beard, if the illustration was to be believed – entitled 'Skankenstein', and promising a 'monstrously slutty time'. Well, now, that sounded interesting, although Jonathan reminded himself that he was engaged – to the charming Mina, no doubt pining for him back in the UK – and that he was here to focus on *business*, namely the restoration of Castle Dragula.

The clip-clopping halted – no, not the sound of heels on the runway, Dear Reader, try to control yourself – but the noise from the exhausted pony that had been dragging the cart for days.

'You're staying with the Cummerbunds, aren't you?' shouted the driver.

'Yes, that's me!' called back Jonathan.

'Well, we're here.'

Jonathan scrambled down from the carriage, catching up his suitcase. Tbh, he was glad to see the back of the villagers. They'd been a strange bunch of travel companions, refusing to play rummikub, shuddering theatrically when he told them he was on his way to Castle Dragula, and constantly trying to ply him with garlic – he presumed as some kind of snack, but he had surreptitiously thrown the cloves out of the window at the first chance he got.

Hopefully the Cummerbunds might be a little more civilised, he thought, as he entered an adorbs thatched cottage, so rustic chic! There was no one to be seen at the reception counter, so he tinged the bell and waited.

After a few minutes, an elderly woman shuffled through. She was as wrinkled as a pair of sweaty tights hastily yanked off, scrunched up and thrown into a corner, thought Jonathan. *Wtf, where did that metaphor even come from?!* Jonathan shook his head. He'd had some pretty weird thoughts ever since he'd entered Transylvania. Like, why were his own clothes so boring, and wouldn't it be nice if there was more glitter in the world? It must have been all that fresh mountain air, and the lashings of local wines with names like Golden Krone – not the best drag name we've ever heard, but Jonathan has to start somewhere.

'Mrs Cummerbund, I presume?' said Jonathan, turning on what he thought was his big-city charm.

The old woman nodded once, scowling.

'Well, dear lady, I am Jonathan Harker – an ambitious young estate agent here to sign off on the reparations of Castle Dragula. I am most wonderfully excited, as I hear the Count is a man of exquisite tastes—'

Mrs Cummerbund winced. 'Sir, please do not speak of Dragula's tastes!'

'Well, why ever not?' asked Jonathan.

She shook her head. 'If you think a Dorito-dusted velour onesie counts as off-duty chic, that's your business. Here's your room key. Oh, and there's a letter for you.' She pushed a note across the reception desk with trembling hands, before disappearing once more.

Rolling his eyes at such nonsensical behaviour, Harker opened the letter, which was from the Count.

BBBBBBZZZZ!

*So excited to have you here in my lands,
FINALLY! Hope the journey not too awful and
some lolz with the villagers possible, they're quite
good fun when you get the party started.*

*Little favour to help a gal out. Can u go to Lil
Bloodsucker's Junk Emporium and pick up a parcel
for ~~me~~ my niece?? It's a corset, size medium, you
can try it if you like!!! Also, get some glue and
tweezers, they need to be strong as these brows are
wiry as fuck.*

*Looking forward to spilling the B — I mean
T!!!!!!! — with you later.*

Love,

 Dragula xoxoxoxoxoxoxo

That's nice, thought Jonathan, even though he had
understood less than a quarter of this rambling letter
and presumed it had come from a frail old man struggling to make himself understood in English. There
was a scrawled order form along with the note, which
Jonathan tucked in his pocket before depositing his
case in his room then setting out for an evening stroll
to find Lil.

It took Jonathan some efforts to persuade the villagers
to guide him to Lil Bloodsucker's, but finally a girl
pointed a trembling and badly manicured finger in the
direction of a cute little stone cottage, the rural idyll

completed by a heavy-set lady of middle age viciously chainsmoking out front.

'Mrs Bloodsucker, I presume?' called Jonathan, tiptoeing his way up the path.

'Who's asking?' she replied in a voice that sounded like something out of *Jurassic Park*, and lit up another cig.

'We haven't been formally introduced, but I am Jonathan Harker, and I am a guest of Count Dragula's. He has asked if I will pick up a parcel for his niece and various other . . . necessities.'

This statement set Lil Bloodsucker off into a hacking laugh that seemed life-threatening, what with all the coughing and spitting that ensued.

'Niece!! *Niece!* Oh that's a good one, come this way, Mr Harker . . . It's trade at least and I don't get much of that nowadays . . .'

Mrs Bloodsucker turned, and Harker followed her ample backside into the shop's interior. It was full of strange wonders – wigs in every hue imaginable, fabrics that seemed to sparkle with a life of their own, strange foam pads – and the shoes! *Oh, the shoes!* Harker's hands trembled and began to move with a power of their own towards a pair of rhinestone platforms, before he snapped out of this bizarre trance.

Mrs Bloodsucker was watching him with interest. 'All alright, Mr Harker?'

Jonathan cleared his throat. 'Yes, fine, thank you.' What had come over him? He forced himself to think about bow ties, worsted wool, a frock coat – frocks! *Jesus, this was difficult.*

Mrs Bloodsucker nodded, seemingly amused. 'Mmmmm child! Now let's see what the old bat wants in this bag of tricks.' She put on a pair of pince-nez and peered at the order form. 'So here we have . . . A corset in a size medium.' She snorted with laughter again. 'With those back rolls . . .'

'Back rolls?' said Jonathan. 'Is that a local delicacy?'

'Not exactly,' said Mrs Bloodsucker, grimacing. 'I'm going to put in an XXL and if she wants to change it she can come down here herself, or she can actually lose some of that weight like she's been talking about for the past century, get back on the runway and do us all a favour. Here, I'm going to put one of these in as well . . .' She handed Jonathan a flyer. 'See if this might tempt her out.'

Jonathan looked at the leaflet. It read:

GHOULS AND BOOS!

Your hairy godmother – that's me, Lil Bloodsucker – invites you to:

VAMPAGEANT: THE RETURN

We welcome all spooks, kooks, merpeople, vampires – INCLUDING YOU, DRAGULA – flora, fauna and toadstools.

ANY BITING MUST BE CONSENSUAL.

What the hell was this? Jonathan supposed it might be something a bit like Morris dancing, and folded the leaflet away.

'And the tweezers . . .' Mrs Bloodsucker threw in a pair of what looked like bolt-cutters. 'And the glue. That comes to 270 guineas.'

'Oh! I presumed the Count would have paid already?'

Wordlessly, Lil turned over the note from the Count and pointed to a scrawl.

WILL PAY U BACK!! PROMISE!

'Well, I presume the Count is a man of his word!' said Harker cheerfully, while Mrs Bloodsucker side-eyed frantically to camera.

•

Jonathan passed a fair night's sleep at the guesthouse, although he was visited by peculiar dreams in which the rhinestone platforms featured prominently – and rather enjoyably. Over breakfast, Mr Cummerbund shuffled in and told Harker that he would continue his journey to castle Dragula by cart until nightfall, whereupon the Count's own carriage would pick him up.

'Oh, but that seems odd,' said Harker, disappointed at the prospect of another bone-rattling stint in peasant class and already acting the diva. 'Why can't the Count collect me for the journey during the day? Particularly given that I am carrying a parcel for his niece.' Jonathan held up the parcel and Mr and Mrs Cummerbund, who had come in to clear away the Mice Krispies, shuddered.

'Mr Harker, sir . . .' began the old man. 'You do understand the nature of the Count?'

'Whatever do you mean?'

Mrs Cummerbund peered around nervously. 'He's not like . . . He's not like the other girls!'

'What on earth do you mean?' said Jonathan, mouth askance and trying to remember the nineteenth-century conventions around gendered pronouns. 'There are . . . young ladies at Castle Dragula?'

There was a loaded silence, during which Mr Cummerbund raised an on-fleek eyebrow and pouted for his life.

'Good sir, there are strange and fantastical goings-on at the castle,' said Mrs Cummerbund breathlessly. 'Howls during the night, flashing lights that cannot come from a humble candle, rumours of—'

'Gurrrl please, say no more, I beg of you!' said Mr Cummerbund, and his wife fell silent.

Jonathan drew himself up tall. 'Good sir, good madam, I have no idea what you are talking about, but I can assure you, I will not hear such licentious gossip against my host! Now *please*, a sandwich for the journey – spelt bread if you have it, a basic sourdough will do if not.'

The couple exchanged a sassy glance and shrugged. Tbh, it would be kind of fine if they avoided another stay from this pompous out-of-towner, whose paprika-induced tummy troubles had caused them to be up since 6 a.m. dealing with the plumbing.

But as they helped Jonathan into the cart, Mrs Cummerbund had a pang of conscience.

'Sir, wait a moment!' She dashed into the guesthouse and back out again.

Harker looked down to see Mrs Cummerbund clutching a pair of hideously ugly, flat, knee-high boots, which she held in a cross shape.

'Please, take them. Wear them for your own sake. They're the only thing that will keep the girls at bay.'

God, whatever, mama, thought Jonathan. He wouldn't be seen dead in these, but his thoughts wandered as if by magic to Mina's delicate footwear; *maybe that with a lace, or even go for a fun Regency realness vibe . . .? Or what about those platforms, eh?*

'Are you alright, Mr Harker?' asked Mrs Cummerbund, noting Jonathan's eyes glaze over.

'Yes, quite alright,' said Harker, clearing his throat and taking the boots with a pinch of his thumb and forefinger.

She nodded. 'Well then, good luck – and don't get slurped up.'

•

Harker's cart wound its way slowly around the perilous Transylvanian roads. When they stopped for a lunch break,

Jonathan chucked the ghastly boots down a ravine, hopefully sending them straight back to hell, where they belonged.

'What do you know of Count Dragula?' Harker asked the driver, a young fellow, clearly of a nervy disposition.

The driver stiffened in fear. 'I don't know anything about that, sir! I don't know anything about the disqualification or whether it were right or wrong.'

'What *are* you talking about?'

The driver blushed furiously. 'Oh god, spoiler alert! I don't know, sir! Some says she's gone mad up there in the castle, that she's dangerous and can't be trusted, but me, I don't know, I don't listen to the gossip if I can help it.'

'But who is this woman? I am asking about Count Dragula! Does he have a madwoman-in-the-attic-type situation?'

The driver shook his head, his eyes wide and bright. 'Sir, you must be careful. In this land, we have our own ways, our own traditions . . . We are watched over by a fierce queen; we do not know when she will make her comeback, but she will not rest until her reputation is known the world over.'

Jonathan nodded. 'I totes get it. It's the same for us with Queen Victoria – who knows where she's going to conquer next!'

Ughhhhhh. Jonathan deserves everything he gets AMIRIGHT? Fret not, plenty of frightful discoveries await him at Castle Dragula, including the unironic wearing of espadrilles.

•

Night began to fall. The wolves howled 'OOOOOOOHHHHHHH GURRRRRRRLLLL! OOOOOOOOH GURRRRRLLLLLL!' in the distance. Harker and his driver were travelling in thick forest now, the trees dark and imposing around them.

'Here you are, sir,' said the nervy driver, pulling the cart up short in a clearing illuminated by the moon. 'I'll leave you here and the Count will collect you.'

'Can you not wait until he has arrived?' asked Jonathan, climbing down.

'No!' The driver threw out Harker's luggage before diving back into the driver's seat and urging the pony on and out of the clearing as fast as possible.

'Well, how very rude,' muttered Jonathan, shivering a little and pulling his collar up in a bid to control a mild sense of panic. The woods were dark and wild, and there was no phone signal to be had for love or money.

A faint jangling caused him to spin round. In a puff of smoke there stood a magnificent coach – gleaming black, drawn by four black horses with legs for days and more plumes of feathers than a carnival queen in Rio de Janeiro. The vibe was quite provincial nightclub – think red velvet seats that were worse for wear and Dragula's Gothic-font initials stamped on every available surface. But Jonathan was delighted, his puzzlement at how he did not hear the coach approach was forgotten in a heartbeat. *This was more like it!* He took a photo and composed a caption for when he could get into signal and gram the shit out of this – *check my new whip, mofux.*

Wordlessly, the driver rose and sashayed down from the carriage, catching up Harker's luggage effortlessly and indicating that he should clamber in. Once Jonathan was seated and faffing about with the complimentary snacks, the driver raised his hand high and clicked his fingers several times before making a downwards zig-zag motion in the air. The horses sprang forward eagerly at his signal. Harker was soon asleep, lulled into the type of relaxation afforded only by close proximity to luxury fabrics.

●

And presently, Dear Reader, we arrive at Castle Dragula itself! We are talking some serious Gothic realness here. A) It's a vast ruined castle. B) There are battlements and buttresses everywhere. C) There is loads of dramatic silhouetting against the moon. D) There are wolves howling. E) The coachman's eyes are glowing red. F) So are the horses'. Need I go on with this kind of lyricism? You get the idea.

Harker awoke and realised he had dribbled a little on the seats. No matter, Jonathan, they have seen far worse. He clambered down from the carriage, which instantly vanished.

He wandered over to an enormous wooden door, but before he could knock, it swung open slowly with a creak. Inside stood a tall old man (although Dragula insists he is 41 and no more), clean-shaven except for a long white moustache that could do with a rethink. He was clad in black from head to foot in the belief that it is slimming, and a pair of espadrilles were unapologetically visible. Cue shiver down the spine – it's Dragula time.

The Count had a strong face with curiously arched nostrils (although he hasn't touched the stuff for three centuries now), a lofty domed forehead and hair growing scantily around the temples but profusely elsewhere – i.e., a shitty wigline. You would not want to get up in that grill and hope to live to tell the tale. I think we all know what I am talking about . . . Yes, it is fangs. But, to be clear, Dragula is totally fabbulussss.

'C-c-c-count Dragula?' stammered Harker.

'Yes, darling, that's me!' called Dragula, waving his fingers coquettishly, instantly giddy with the forgotten buzz of recognition. 'I am delighted to see my reputation precedes me! But come in, come in – there's a free shot before midnight.'

Dragula waited with bated breath as Jonathan tiptoed over the threshold to the castle. The door slammed shut and lots of dry ice billowed up, causing Jonathan to bend over, coughing. Dragula cackled manically before clamping his hands over his mouth.

'Muhahhahaha, muhahhahaha – sorry, I get nervous sometimes. I'm not used to meet 'n greets any more. But welcome, darling, to Castle Dragula! You must need to eat and rest. I will leave you to untuck, I mean unpack, in the jugular contusions lounge.'

Dragula let out another giggle at this last remark, which bounced sonorously around the walls, causing a flurry of bats to flutter down towards Harker, who dropped to his knees in terror.

'Dragula! Get them away! They're in my hair, oh, my hair!'

'Darling, calm down,' Dragula cried out. 'I can lend you a wig if anything terribly untoward happens, but look, they're heading out already!'

Harker glanced up to see the bats streaming out of a window.

'Those crazy kids,' said Dragula fondly. 'Now come along, get up off your knees – far too early for those kind of antics, especially on a school night.'

'Dragula, I am Jonathan Harker,' said Harker carefully, wary of the old man's sanity – he seemed to think Jonathan was some gentleman by the name of Darling. 'I am here from Cockstons of London, to arrange the refurb we discussed.'

'Yes yes, darling, I know!' replied Dragula. Jonathan didn't have the heart to correct him yet again. Dragula insisted on carrying Harker's cases along the corridor, then up a great winding staircase and along another passage, hewn from thick stone. Dragua clicked his fingers and the candles lining the corridor sprang into life.

'Neat trick, no?' Dragula said. 'My goodness, Mr Harker, these cases are heavy – I must enquire quite how many pairs of heels you have brought with you?!'

'Count, the extra weight is doubtless due to the package I am carrying on behalf of your good niece,' snapped back Harker, suddenly quite the little bitch.

Dragula paused and turned round, a frown of confusion knitting those mighty brows together. 'Niece? What on earth are you banging on about?'

Harker spoke patiently, now entirely convinced that Dragula was demented. 'Yes indeed, Count, for whom I procured the l-l-ladies' undergarments in the village. And the tweezers, I can only presume.'

'Ah yes, yes, NIECE, now I understand you, well, she's away for the foreseeable future, so I'll just take these for safekeeping, don't you worry,' said Dragula, adding in an innocent whistle for good measure.

'The lady at the shop said a size XXL corset was necessary,' said Jonathan cattily. *Where was this new attitude coming from?* he wondered. It was hardly the conduct of a gentleman.

Dragula sucked his stomach in and consequently his voice was a little more strained than usual. 'The lady at the shop is a jealous old shoeleather. Bloodsucker by name, bloodsucking bitch by nature!'

Dragula whipped back around and headed off at a pace, muttering under his breath about natural metabolism. He showed Harker to a bedroom, before huffing off to do some core stability exercises in the dungeon – though somehow this always turned into eating Doritos and watching videos of kittens on Youtube.

The room once would have been glorious but was now suffering a little from a sense of faded grandeur – there was a distinct smell of mildew and it's probably best not to enquire when the sheets were last changed. Still, there were some ornate brocade drapes to provide some genuine eleganza, and a fire roaring in the corner, plus a four-poster bed complete with signed photo of Dragula on the bedside table. Jonathan got changed – alas not into his heels, more boring nineteenth-century wool worsted vibes – and went to join Dragula for dinner.

•

Although there were places set for two, Dragula did not eat and consumed only a skinny bitch vodka and tonic. He was piqued by the XXL corset and resolved to return it immediately. Well, or once a few pounds had been lost. Maybe it was time to restart the liquids-only diet of yore . . .

Noticing the Count lost in thought, Jonathan tried to steer the conversation back to the renovations of Castle Dragula itself.

'Count, I was admiring the buttresses when I arrived,' said Jonathan, chewing on something gristly that may or may not have been bat-au-vin.

Dragula wiggled his hips. 'Mr Harker, you saucy minx!'

Jonathan blushed, although he wasn't quite sure why. 'Would it be possible to take a tour later?'

Dragula fixed him with a steely gaze. 'I'm sorry, my dear, but you're not really my type. Oh, you mean the *castle!*'

At this, the Count became grave. 'Jonathan, I must warn you. I have rendered these quarters safe for your habitation, but you must not wander throughout, particularly into the VIP or backstage areas. It would not be safe for you. I have locked the doors accordingly and you must not attempt to venture further – it is for your own good.'

Jonathan nodded slowly.

'Oh, also, don't look in any wardrobes,' added Dragula, before leaning in and whispering into Jonathan's ear, 'I don't think you're ready for this jelly.'

•

The first few days of Jonathan's stay at Castle D weren't too bad. There are a couple of weird things to note, though. He frequently discovered long strands of hair in multitudes of colours (some most unnatural), when there were no women in Castle Dragula. Furthermore,

Jonathan never saw the Count in the day, but at night they often stayed up late in the library. Dragula liked to tell Jonathan rambling tales of the 80s – that's the 1880s.

'A career in TV, now that's difficult,' said Dragula, sparking up another cig and struggling to hold it in place and talk, given those fangs.

'TV?' queried Jonathan, barely conscious after being plied with yet another of Dragula's potent Bloody Marys.

'TV – Transylvania! It used to be the place to be! Everyone who was *anyone* tried to make it here. The village was where Nosferatutu first debuted her interpretative dance performance of *The Nutcracker*, by Tights-Off-Sky! What a time to be living! But, oh, Jonathan, things change . . .'

Dragula paused, a host of memories flooding back, and shook his head. 'This bloody business we call show, Jonathan. One slip-up, one tiny little mistake, and you're dead. It's lethal.'

But Jonathan was already fast asleep, and Dragula's words went unheeded.

•

Rising late one afternoon after another all-nighter with the Count, Jonathan was dismayed to find that the brocade drapings in his bedroom had been badly damaged, with large pieces of fabric slashed out of them. Fearing that the Count would think he had trashed his room,

Harker went to find him, eventually locating Dragula in the library snipping out illustrations from *Vogue* and pretending not to have just devoured a family-sized pack of Monster Munch.

'Good day, sir!' said Jonathan brightly. 'Or I suppose evening may be more appropriate, given that nightfall is already upon us. Does it ever get light around here?'

'Not if I can help it,' muttered Dragula. 'Far better to exist only in the kindness of candlelight, my dear.'

'Well, anyway, something strange has happened,' continued Jonathan, twisting his hands nervously. 'The brocade drapes in my room – they've been massacred! Big slashes cut out of them! I assure you it was nothing I did, but the damage is substantial.'

The Count waved an arm dismissively. 'Don't worry about it, Mr Harker. I can assure you it's all for a good cause.'

This was not what Jonathan was expecting. The Count's reactions were difficult to predict – only the previous evening at dinner, Dragula had gone off in a huff when Harker had mentioned that garlic was good for the immune system. But now the Count seemed meek and mild, and so Jonathan attempted to garner some brownie points. 'Perhaps some wild animal gained admittance and became tangled in the drapes, damaging them in its bid for freedom? A Venetian shutter may help keep them from the castle interiors, I'm sure I have a brochure . . .'

Dragula snorted. 'Wild animals! You could say that,

the girls do need to learn how to behave, although I'm not sure throwing a poor Venetian at them is the way to do it.'

'The girls? Your niece, she is returned?'

Jesus Christ, he is sticking to this story, thought Dragula impatiently. 'No, she's still away on her gap year, Jonathan.'

'Ah! Do you have other family, Count?'

Dragula paused theatrically, ever the professional. 'Not in the sense you would presently understand, Mr Harker. But I do have those I consider to be . . . daughters.'

Dragula locked eyes with the camera and the scene faded to black.

•

You'd think Harker would pick up on such clangers, but no. Instead, he went back to his shredded-up quarters and decided to have a shave while considering his options. The Count didn't seem particularly interested in Jonathan's plans for renovations, and Harker needed that commission like knees need moisturising. Maybe it was time to give up on this one and get back to life with Mina.

His thoughts were interrupted by a claw-like grip around the throat.

'*How do you get the shave so close?*' Dragula hissed,

running his finger down Jonathan's cheek. 'It's so smooth! So very very smooth!'

Unable to breathe, Jonathan managed a small squeak.

'Tell me your secret!' raged the Count, his grip growing ever tighter.

Jonathan hadn't seen this kind of temper from the Count before, but such an outburst will come as no surprise to veterans of the TV scene, where Dragula's tantrums were the stuff of legend.

Wordlessly, Jonathan managed to raise the razor and the Count snatched it from his trembling fingers.

'What a clever little thing!' he cooed, turning it over and reading the brand. 'Lady Shaver? Well, now I never, I wondered where the old girl had gone and clearly she's been putting her wits to good use if this is what she's come up with!'

Jonathan was wheezing on the floor, although somewhere at the back of his mind he wondered how he didn't see the Count's approach in the shaving mirror.

'Can I keep it, Jonathan? Please? Please?'

Jonathan nodded, too afraid to protest otherwise, but the Count was now in an excellent humour and even brought Jonathan a honey and lemon to help with the sore throat.

'Sorry about that, Mr Harker! Touch of the nerves. The pressure at the top is quite something. Anyhow, the little razor is much appreciated, and I also want to say that I think it's best you stay in your quarters tonight – wouldn't want you to get under anyone's feet or anything . . .'

Jonathan nodded obediently and drained his honey and lemon, which made him curiously drowsy . . .

•

He awoke several hours later and the moon was high – not the only thing that's high in Castle Dragula atm, let me tell you that for nothing. Desperate for a glass of water, Jonathan tumbled out of bed and staggered about looking for a tap or a pitcher in his quarters, throwing open cupboards and wardrobes willy-nilly, out of which tumbled dozens of mismatched heels, two plastic flamingos and an abundance of statement earrings.

A rage rose up in our mild Mr Harker. *What the hell was Dragula playing at?* Dragging him all the way to Transylvania, when he's clearly no interest in the renovations, keeping Jonathan awake all hours banging on about showbiz, asking if he's interested in the merch, nicking his razor – oh, and he still hadn't paid him back for that bloody corset. Enough is enough! Surely there was a night bus back to Tuckerweiner, from where he could get the hell out of here on the next Wizzair flight back to London? Jonathan strode downstairs and pulled open the castle door. Only, it wouldn't open. Jonathan tugged again, before concluding that the door was definitely locked. He tried a window. Also locked.

Panicking, he began to run, trying any door that looked like it might lead, well, anywhere. They were all locked! Heart pounding, Jonathan realised he was effectively a prisoner here. What exactly did the Count have planned for him? Did the blethering villagers have a point after all? What was it they'd said about slurpings and fierce queens? Jonathan returned to his room and was trying to force himself to think calmly when he heard a piercing shriek and some demonic cackling.

Other prisoners! thought Jonathan. *I must find them, together we can overpower Dragula and make our escape!*

With strengthened resolve, Jonathan began his journey through the depths of the castle, trying to follow the direction from which he heard the shrieking, although things had now fallen ominously silent. Lost in a maze of moonlit corridors, eventually he wandered into what appeared to be a ladies' drawing room, replete with chaise longues, tasteful soft furnishings and loads of crinolines chucked about the place.

Exhausted by the adrenaline, and still no further with his escape plans, Jonathan sat down on the couch and instantly fell asleep again – clearly Dragula's honey and lemon recipe was rather potent.

•

Jonathan woke again with a start. In the spotlight, sorry moonlight, he saw three young women dressed in flowing black gowns. *Am I still dreaming?* wondered Jonathan. Although the moonlight was behind the women, they threw no shadow. They were, however, capable of throwing plenty of shade.

Jonathan was relieved. Thank God, finally some allies to aid the escape from Dragula's clutches – and rather pretty ones at that, although he quickly batted that thought away.

'Ladies, fear not! I have come to rescue you from Count Dragula! We must all remain calm and keep together, and we will soon be out of his dastardly clutches.'

The three girls linked hands and skipped in a circle, cackling wildly. Jonathan felt rather discombobulated. This wasn't the usual conduct of noble ladies. He studied them more closely. Two were dark-haired, with the same 'challenging' brow structure as Dragula, and the other was a wispy blonde. They all had ruby-red lips and strangely pointed white teeth, and their eyes burned brightly, framed with thick luxurious lashes, the likes of which Jonathan had never seen before.

'Rescue us from Mother? Good luck with that!' chirped one of the dark-haired girls, before going over to the window, folding her arms and staring out of it moodily.

'From *Mother*?' breathed Jonathan.

'Yes!' said the other dark-haired girl. 'For we are the Daughters of the House of Dragula! I am Fangela, that's Edwina Sullen sulking over there, and the stringy blonde is Lilith Paltrow.'

Lilith smiled dreamily. 'You may have heard of my lifestyle blog.'

'An addiction to sun-in and using the Dorito dust from Dragula's latest binge as a nasty bronzer doth not a valley girl make,' muttered Edwina from the window. 'And don't let her start selling you one of her colonics.'

'There's no need for you, darling, you're already far enough up your own arse as it is,' said Lilith, nonetheless rubbing at her hairline which was indeed quite orange. 'And if you're not careful I'll shove a jade egg down your throat again.'

Jonathan rubbed his eyes, convinced he was dreaming. 'The Daughters of . . . But the Count said he had no daughters . . .'

Fangela scowled. 'Typical! She's always so hard on us! She's no *idea* what it's like being in the House of Dragula. Oh, it used to mean something alright, but nowadays, it's a bloody joke.'

'What on earth do you mean?'

'You know, what happened between Dragula and Van High Heelsing? Why we're in this whole sorry mess?'

Jonathan shook his head, too dumbfounded to speak.

Fangela and Lilith sighed, and moved to sit either side of him. 'Looks like we need to start from the beginning, Fangela. Settle down, Jonathan, it's time for a backstory.'

Fangela nodded, and began the tale.

'So, once upon a time, believe it or not, Transylvania was the place to be, the epicentre of the drag universe. And no one was more legendary than Dragula and her BFF, Babebraham Van High Heelsing – straight from Amsterdam, fishier than a North Sea herring boat. Those two had the scene sewn up between them. Dragula was famous for her avant-garde act, her costumes – and especially her lip syncs, the fangs weren't as overgrown then, but rather added a certain . . . *edge* to the proceedings. And the villagers loved her. Yes, she had a temper on her but it was because she *cared* so much, because she *wanted* it so much. Sometimes her act wouldn't work out, but she always took that risk – and when it did work, it was out of this world. Van High Heelsing was different. She was a looker, alright, think Amsterdam Red Light District realness – all body and fetishwear and big blond hair. She had talent, too, to be fair. She could nail a lip sync, she could dance like a pair of pythons in silk pyjamas, but she wasn't as original as Dragula. So Dragula would help her with costumes, with new ideas for her routines, and they got along famously.'

'Van High Heelsing was always a bitch to her,' sniffed Edwina from the window. 'Always coming out with fad diets for Dragula to try, like that blood one, or negging her about her eyebrows – I mean, Dragula is *all about* the power brow.'

Lilith nodded her agreement. 'That's true, but we didn't see it then. We were young queens just starting out, I was a woodcutter's son back then, and my – I did not know what the fuck I was doing! I had to carve my first pair of heels from a pine tree! So we just idolised those two – and the day we finally joined the House of Dragula was the best of my life. We could have joined Van High Heelsing . . .'

'We still could!' piped up Edwina. 'God knows we might actually see some action with her rather than witnessing Dragula's daily descent into an eternity of elasticated waists.'

'Edwina, how could you?! Have a little faith,' scolded Lilith.

Fangela continued the story. 'So one day a new competition was announced by Lil Bloodsucker – the VAMPageant! We were thrilled! Preparations were fierce, drag fans from all over the world flooded to Transylvania to see the competition – it was a wonderful time. We all thought Dragula would win, and, of course, she did. She did this amazing trick where she walked like a lizard up the walls and whooshed down with this surprise cape unfolded, my, it was incredible!' The Daughters cooed at the memory.

'The thing about Dragula is that she was always herself. She always stood up and dared to be different, and that's why she won,' said Edwina, unfolding her arms momentarily, which was as close as she got to displaying positive emotion.

'But Van High Heelsing . . . We didn't know what she was capable of. When it came to Dragula's crowning ceremony, she completely sabotaged her. She'd been spreading rumours about Dragula's capacity to represent the Transylvania drag community on a global platform – hints that Dragula was too unpredictable, too emotional, to fulfil her duties. At the ceremony, Dragula stepped forward to walk the runway and be crowned – and Van High Heelsing pulled down the drapes that covered the windows of the barn, lit favourably with candles, so that Dragula was struck with the horrors of the first rays of sunlight. As any drag queen would be, Dragula was terrified – there is *nothing* as unforgiving as harsh natural daylight – and she threw up her hands to cover her face! Taking advantage of Dragula's panic, Van High Heelsing bowled a bulb of garlic – traditionally thrown by the peasants as a sign of their appreciation and approval – under Dragula's heels, causing her to stack it in spectacular style all over the runway.

'Suffice to say, Dragula. Lost. Her. Shit. She glanced up and saw the smirk on Van High Heelsing's face as she scuttled back to her position as first runner-up, and launched herself at her former BFF. Van High Heelsing didn't even fight back! She just kept squeaking for help and saying that Dragula was biting her neck, until Dragula was hauled off by Lil. Anyway, Dragula was stripped of her crown and title, which was handed to Van High Heelsing. And as a further punishment for the alleged biting, Lil condemned Dragula to be unable to see her own reflection in the mirror until she had that temper under control.'

'Dragula left the scene in floods of tears, her reputation shot to pieces and her rightful crown perched atop the cheap peroxide tresses of a friend she had trusted with everything. She's been planning a comeback ever since, a bid to restore the name of the House of Dragula, but . . . it's hard. She can't practise new looks easily. The villagers are suspicious – some are scared of her – so she stays away most of the time. She's kind of lost her confidence.'

'And it's hard for us, too! We joined the House of Dragula to be legendary, not stuck in some draughty old castle for all eternity,' growled Lilith, suddenly restless. 'But you, Mr Harker, you could provide a little entertainment for us!'

Fangela clapped her hands. 'Oh yes! What are you thinking, dear sister?'

'I'm thinking a little makeover challenge! And then perhaps a healthy snack . . .'

Lilith was now peering at Jonathan just as a cat stares at a mouse, and the hairs on the back of his neck stood on end. This would not do! As a man, it was up to him to quell these crazed ramblings and get them all away from Dragula's clutches. What nonsense these girls were spouting, clearly they were in the grip of some feminine moon-induced madness!

'L-l-ladies!' began Jonathan, attempting to rise but unceremoniously shoved back down by Fangela. My, she was strong for a lady! 'Please, I need you all to come to your senses and we will make our escape from the castle and—'

'What are you going to do, Lilith?' said Fangela.

'I'm not sure, I think something classy yet sexy, you know, noblewoman on the streets, freaky in the sheets,' replied Lilith, tracing a finger down Jonathan's cheek, which made him shiver.

Fangela rolled her eyes. 'Boring.'

'Oh, what do you want to do?'

'Something different! I mean, a nautical look or something?'

Lilith broke out in vicious giggles, and Edwina joined in from the window. She walked over to Jonathan and leant over him, arching her back in a most unladylike but nonetheless appealing fashion, and licking her lips.

'Nautical,' drawled Edwina. 'You and your stripes, Fangela. This isn't bloody *Beetlejuice*.'

Fangela snarled at her sister, causing Jonathan to start.

'Hush hush, ladies, please. You're frightening him!' purred Lilith. 'We can start gently. Is it your first time, Jonathan?'

She fixed Harker with her sapphire-blue eyes, and Jonathan found himself as if hypnotised. He closed his eyes and allowed himself to fall into Lilith's icy embrace. He could feel her drawing nearer and nearer, her breath cool against his cheek, oh but surely he must put a stop to these dastardly games and suggest something more soothing, billiards perhaps? Things looked to be getting quite out of control . . .

With a superhuman effort he wrenched open his eyes and saw Lilith with her red lips agape, white teeth glinting, a small tube of lipstick bared as she applied another coating of the House of Dragula's signature lip colour, Vampire's Kiss.

'You next, my dear,' said Lilith, and she moved closer to Jonathan. 'Now try not to wriggle or you'll smudge this terribly.'

Jonathan lay unable to move, gripped by the combination of terror and desire that generally surfaces at 3 a.m. He shut his eyes in fright as Lilith drew nearer, and felt her lips brush his own –

'No! No!' cried Jonathan, thrashing his head from side to side and causing Lilith to smear red lipstick all over his face and teeth, so that everything began to look rather gory indeed.

'Now look what you've done, you've ruined it!' hissed Lilith, grabbing Jonathan's neck in a vice-like grip and squeezing. 'You. Will. Stay. Still!'

The sisters cheered from the sidelines. *What is it with Castle Dragula and throats*, thought Jonathan, gasping for air, convinced he had met his doom, when *whoomph* – Lilith was knocked away from him and onto the floor.

Panting, Jonathan gazed upon his saviour. She was an extraordinary-looking woman, dressed in a floor-length brocade gown – the fabric of which looked remarkably familiar – and a sweeping black cape with a high collar. Her hair was long and jet black except for a single white streak, and her complexion was startlingly pale, with heavy dark brows and brilliant crimson lips.

'Girls! If I've told you once, I've told you a thousand times, leave him alone! No meddling in my property!'

She waved a bejewelled hand and the three sisters cowered back.

'We're sorry, Mother! We didn't mean to!' simpered Lilith.

'It's just I'm so *bored*, all the time,' added Edwina Sullen, her arms folded across her chest and eyes downcast.

'Me too!' said Fangela, picking uncouthsomely at her long canines. 'How can you expect me to lip sync with teeth like this?'

'Indeed, sister! Or practise new looks when we can't see our reflections!' mewed Lilith.

Dragula – for it is she, clever reader – felt exhausted. These spoiled little bitches, so ungrateful for the opportunities – and admittedly unique set of challenges – afforded by the House of Dragula. Why couldn't they just learn to uphold the legend, support her in making a showstopping comeback, allow her to retire with some lucrative merchandising deals, and then carry on the Dragula legacy? Was it really so much to fucking ask?

Dragula paced over to the window and sparked up a cig, staring out at the Transylvanian landscape. God it was lonely at the top. At times like this, she could also bring herself to miss Van High Heelsing, but no – that bitch. She was raking it in all over the place now, ensconced in her canal house complete with sexy dungeon *and* smart lighting. Dragula secretly followed her on Instagram, under a pseudonym account, and occasionally posted comments like, 'I hate your hair' and 'that wallpaper shrivels my soul'.

The squabble between the Daughters gathered pace. Dragula turned, taking in the fact that Jonathan was lolling about on the sofa in a semi-swoon and being utterly useless. She'd entertained brief thoughts of trying to draw him into the House of Dragula – he'd be fishy, no doubt about it – but his irritating personality and general lack of talent made that a no-no. Dragula walked over to the chaise longue, loosening her corsets and tugging off her wig.

Jonathan shrieked in horror at the emergence of that distinctive hairline.

Dragula glared at him. 'Pipe down, Jonathan, you've had enough hints.'

The quarrel between the Daughters was showing no signs of slowing down, and every sign of getting physical. Dragula took the opportunity to slip into a relaxing floor-length kaftan and pop open a tube of Pringles.

'Girls!' Dragula clapped her hands. 'Calm yourselves! We will practise a category, it will be—'

'CAPE!' they screeched in unison. 'Same as forever! CAPE, CAPE, CAPE!'

Dragula was appalled. Such disrespect for the signature silhouette!

'We just want to try something else!' sobbed Edwina, ever the drama queen.

'Please, Dragula! Just something a little bit different!' pleaded Lilith, hands clasped beseechingly.

Dragula sighed and frankly couldn't be arsed with the argument. Maybe the girls had a point. There had been a lot of cape over the past few years.

'Fine! We will practise lip-syncing to the wolves' howls.'

The girls still looked surly. Dragula looked around for further inspiration.

'And you can drink Jonathan, if you really want.'

Delighted, the Daughters sprang forth. 'Oh, thank you, Mother, thank you!'

'It's so good for the complexion.' Lilith smiled, baring her fangs happily.

Jonathan squeaked and tried to wriggle into the chaise longue.

'Dragula, please! Not this! I have a fiancée back in London, I have so much to live for! And what about the plans for an en suite in the master bedroom?'

Dragula shrugged. 'I'm sorry, my dear, but you are up for digestion. But do not worry, your death won't be in vain!' She pointed to her top lip. 'See, the moustache is all gone! Your little razor isn't afraid of hard work, is she? I will think fondly of you every time I use it, dear Mr Harker.'

The Daughters crowded closer to Jonathan, licking their lips.

'Just mind the upholstery please, girls,' said Dragula, moving away.

'Please, let me gaze upon the visage of my dear Mina just one last time,' begged Jonathan, and Dragula nodded. She was a softie underneath it all.

Jonathan rummaged in his pocket and pulled out a photo of Mina, standing with her cousin Lukie Westenra.

'Ooh, who's that?' said Fangela. 'Look at her hair! Is that the fashion?'

'Give it to me!' said Edwina, snatching it away, before Lilith pulled her hair and grabbed the photo back, all thoughts of drinking Jonathan disappearing in this new squabble.

'For fuck's sake,' muttered Dragula, snapping her fingers and indicating that Lilith should deposit the photo in her hands, which she sulkily did.

Dragula glanced down at the photo, and felt her heart leap.

'Jonathan! Jonathan! Who is this?'

'It's Mina, my darling . . .' he croaked.

'No! The divine creature next to her.' Dragula stroked the image with a painted fingernail.

Jonathan peered at the photo. 'Ah! That's Lukie Westenra, Mina's cousin.'

'And you know this boy?'

'Yes! He will be family once we are wed.'

'And where does Lukie reside?'

'Whitby, presently. A seaside town in the north of England.'

Dragula walked over to the window, with the photo, lost in thought. Was she imagining things? She glanced again at the picture. No, there was something there. The obvious sass, the tilt to the jawline, the way in which the cape was angled and worn with clear passion – and Dragula had always had a talent for finding new blood. Could this be the reason the fates had brought Jonathan Harker to Transylvania? To lead Dragula to a worthy successor to the House of Dragula . . . Perhaps it was worth keeping him alive after all . . .

•

Jonathan awoke back in his familiar quarters. Judging from the calls of the birds outside and the sun streaming in at the window, it must be early afternoon. What a bizarre dream he'd had last night! Outlandish women, an attempt on his life, and most fantastical of all – a red lipstick with the staying power of eternity! Thank goodness this was revealed to be a fiction, apart from the lipstick, which would admittedly be damn useful, but he resolved to leave Castle Dragula immediately – clearly the place was having an effect on his sanity. Jonathan rolled out of bed, intent on informing the Count that he would be leaving post-haste.

Jonathan wandered through the castle, now silent and tranquil in daylight.

'Count?' he called. Surely the old man must be awake by now.

He peered in all the doors he could find, which now opened easily. He found a door that opened to a stair-case, spiralling down into the castle depths. Tentatively, Jonathan made his way down the stairs, which led to a heavy oak door. Jonathan pushed this open and screamed with the shock.

Inside the room was an open coffin, and slumped halfway into it, having passed out unceremoniously in the small hours, was the Count! The Count's eyes were glassy and unfocused, the complexion pale and clammy, the lips smeared red and there was a reek of strong spirits throughout the room. Dragula's eyes opened further, bloodshot and bleary, and the Count attempted to croak something to Jonathan, accompanied by a pointing finger.

Dear Reader, you no doubt correctly recognise this state of living death as that of a drastic hangover, and would have answered Dragula's incoherent plea for water and Berocca, but our Mr Harker decided this was another attempt on his life, and threw his hands up to his mouth in campy horror. (For a newbie, he is learning fast, no?) The aforementioned hands came away smeared a brilliant red! Jonathan screamed! Last night had all been real, and provided a salutary lesson in the importance of taking off your make-up before bedtime.

Unwilling to face some basic truths about skincare, Harker fled up the stairs and flung himself at the front door, then out into the wilds of Transylvania.

Oh well, thought Dragula, trying to ignore the pounding headache and sense of existential dread, and instead snuggling back down into the coffin, which was ever so effective at relieving lower back pain. Whitby, eh? Maybe it was time to take the girls for a little sea air – and to meet their new sister . . .

PART TWO

Dearest Reader, are you still with me?
Because now we're heading to the town of Whitby,
Where we'll meet Mina and her fair cousin,
Upon whose cheekbones Dragula is crushing.
Lukie's unaware of the transformation that awaits,
Involving curling tongs, padding and swaying gaits,
There's much to learn when it comes to nipping and tucking,
Plus he'll need those eyebrows plucking.
Thankfully Dragula is a dab hand with the tweezers,
Long-practised upon Transylvania's rural geezers.
I can't think of any more rhymes now,
So let's crack on.

Mina and her cousin Lukie were strolling along the sea-front in the chronically under-appreciated northern seaside town of Whitby, and gossiping about Lukie's torrid love life like a pair of cawing seagulls. Mina felt a bit jealous when she heard of the hotties that Lukie was presently juggling, which included both a Texan AND the head of an insane asylum. What bants! Yeah, she had Jonathan, but sometimes she thought he was a bit basic and wondered if the sparkle was going out of their relationship before they'd even been wed.

Oh yes, talking of Jonathan, Mina realised she hadn't heard from him for a while, but a strange letter had arrived supposedly in his hand, asking her to start making some dresses that aren't even in her size. She mentioned this to Lukie, and asked if she should be worried.

'Nah, it's probably fine,' said Lukie, shrugging, before grabbing Mina's arm and pointing at the horizon. 'Look! What's that?'

A cruise liner was approaching through the waves, its heavy silhouette outlined against the sunset and disco lights flashing from all portholes. They could just about make out its name, the *Kween Elizabeth 2* (even though, yes, she hasn't been born, but whatever . . .).

Mina frowned. 'It looks like some kind of pleasure tour. But how unusual that it would be docking in Whitby . . .'

'Come on, let's go and see what's happening,' said Lukie, flipping his cape elegantly around his shoulders and offering Mina his arm.

They followed the liner's progress up into the harbour, where the ship moored and the passengers began to disembark. They all looked rather strange – pale as if they were exhausted, and yet glossy-eyed and elated, and many – including the ship's captain – with bright red lips.

'Eee, it were fantastic,' said an elderly man to Lukie as he wobbled down the gangplank. 'Me and the wife, we've never seen on-board ents like it! Started a bit late, mind, but those girls! They were out of this world! They were a-singing, they were a-dancing. It beats that whale-watching trip we did last time, that's for sure, although don't let Dragula hear me talking about whales, I know she's a bit self-conscious about her weight – nearly took that fella's arm off when he asked if there'd be the opportunity to land a big fish . . .'

Mina and Lukie exchanged a bemused glance.

'Shame they lost our luggage, though,' continued the old man.

'It weren't lost, sir,' piped up a sailor, also daubed with the signature red and wearing a nautically striped crop top. 'We had to make way for a special cargo – fifty crates of false eyelashes from Transylvania.'

'Ooh, well then, that were all in a good cause!' said the old man, before turning to Lukie and Mina. 'You two need to book yourself on the next one! You'll have the time of your life!'

Any further conversation was cut off by a huge black dog that bounded down the gangplank, swiftly followed by three bats that appeared to be squabbling. This is a textbook trick of Dragula's to avoid any tricky moments at passport control, and taxation questions about earnings in cash.

•

Up in the ruins of Whitby Abbey, Dragula and the Daughters made themselves right at home.

'See, girls, it's just like the castle!' said Dragula cheerily. The abbey had admittedly looked different online, but don't we all? The lack of a roof posed a bit of a problem, but Dragula managed to convince the girls that this was all part of the authentic retreat he'd booked them on, where they would refresh and replenish both body and mind.

'It's to do with fresh air and feng shui,' Dragula announced, slipping into a monogrammed dressing gown and a pair of espadrilles.

'Where's the spa?' said Lilith, looking round with her nose turned up. 'You said we were going on holiday and that there would be a spa.'

'My dear, the point of this very exclusive retreat is that . . . the spa is a state of *mind*. Where isn't the spa, is the question. You must meditate on the jacuzzi until you *are* the jacuzzi, yes?'

Lilith seemed satisfied by this. God she was quite stupid sometimes, reflected Dragula. But no matter, there were more important matters to contend with and werk to be done!

'Did you see Lukie?' said Dragula, squeaking like a bat with excitement. 'Right when we got off the boat? Now, girls, *that* is how to wear a cape with attitude!'

The Daughters fell into a sulk. 'I hope you're not going to make her your new favourite,' said Edwina.

'Darlings, I don't have favourites,' said Dragula, aware that this was a massive lie. 'But we need a little bit of fresh talent to pep things up, and I think Lukie could be it. Then we can return *in triumph* to the Transylvania scene! Look, I have something to show you. But no snapping!'

The Daughters gathered round Dragula, who pulled out the tattered VAMPageant leaflet and held it aloft for the girls to see.

'Ladies, I think we are ready. It's time to rise from the dead and slay on the runway.'

'You can take back the crown, Dragula! And we can walk again, we can finally walk!' cried Fangela, taking her sisters' hands and hopping up and down.

'Yes, that's the plan,' said Dragula, heartened by the girls' enthusiasm. 'But we must prepare well. We've been in the shadows a long time, and a lacklustre comeback from the dead would finish off the House of Dragula once and for all. Lukie must be prepared, too. We need to begin to visit Lukie, we must call him to us, tempt him in – make sure he is really committed to this. Then – and only then – can we start his transformation! And, girls, we must operate with the utmost secrecy. If Van High Heelsing hears we are planning our comeback, there's no telling what she would do to hold on to her crown.'

The Daughters shuddered.

'But first, let us dine,' said Dragula, lightening the mood. 'Do you think the ents staff are still locked in the engine room?'

•

The following morning, Lukie descended to breakfast looking absolutely exhausted.

'Why, Lukie, you look like you haven't slept a wink! Have you been sneaking out to see your Texan again?' said Mina, pouring her cousin a cup of coffee.

Lukie slumped down at the kitchen table, rubbing at the deep shadows under his eyes. 'No, it wasn't Quincy. I had the strangest night – I don't know if I was asleep or awake. I heard strange howls, and then I was visited by bizarre dreams – a lady with sharp teeth and enormous hair, with three daughters, all singing and dancing in unison and calling me to them. And I think I must have walked in my sleep, for when I awoke properly, I was turning the key in the front door, as if I was about to leave!'

Mina placed her palm on Lukie's forehead. 'It could be that you have a fever, dear cousin. Best take it easy today and hope for a good night's sleep tonight.'

•

But, oh my dears, this was only the start of a bizarre series of events in Whitby. The newspaper reported that an old man had been found with his neck broken at the bottom of the steps up to the ruined abbey, with a pair of platform heels nearby – clearly too much for him to handle on a first outing. Rumours spread of three sisters painting the town's lips red – yes, the girls were plying their nautical makeovers to any sailor who chanced to find himself alone in a dark alley late at night.

Mina grew more concerned about Lukie. For several nights now she'd discovered him sleepwalking through the house – the previous evening, she'd been woken up by him rummaging through her wardrobe, in a trance. She'd guided him back to bed, confused by his quite lucid questions about corsets. These nocturnal meanderings exhausted him, meaning he slept all day and surfaced only at twilight. Mina supposed he must need the rest, but hoped this strange fever would soon break.

A week after the cruise ship had docked in Whitby, Mina woke with a start at 3 a.m. Was that the front door she had heard bang? Quickly, she ran to the window and peered out. Lukie! He was dancing nimbly up the street, making mysterious rhythmic gestures with his arms that looked, frankly, amazing.

Mina threw on a shawl and hurried downstairs and out of the cottage, determined to follow her cousin, but he moved so quickly in this state, even though . . . were those her *shoes* he was tripping about so elegantly in? Lukie picked up the pace and sprang away ahead of her around a corner, and she lost sight of him.

'Damn!' cursed Mina, worried for her cousin's safety. She paused and listened. Yes, there! The unmistakable tapping of heels on cobblestones. She gathered up her skirts and ran on through the deserted streets, in the direction of the sound. She arrived at the base of the steps to the ruined abbey. There was Lukie, illuminated by moonlight, strutting sassily up the steps and pausing only to lean back on the railing, with one leg stretched out, the other kicked back, and blowing kisses to the night sky.

What strange sickness is this? pondered Mina. *And where can I catch it?*

We'll be touring soon, came a voice in her head. *Love Dragula.*

Mina shook her head from side to side, clearing her thoughts, and dashed up the steps as fast as she could. Panting, she reached the top, and there, lit by the flattering light of the moon and reclining coquettishly on a tumbled-down gravestone, was Lukie! Was that a *dress* of hers he was clutching? Never mind *that* – there was also a shadowy figure, wearing a cape with a high-necked collar, leaning over her cousin and brandishing a tiny gold tube containing a bright scarlet substance. What devilry was this? Mina cried out and the creature glanced up, giving her a glimpse of a white face and red gleaming eyes. Yes, Dear Reader, we can conclude from this sighting that Dragula has not learned to contour on the way over.

'Brb!' called the shadowy figure, fleeing away with unnatural speed.

Mina rushed over to her cousin. 'Lukie! Lukie! Are you alright?'

Lukie smiled at her beatifically, eyes blank and glassy. 'I'm quite alright, Mina. In fact, I've never been better.' He gazed at her, and began to mouth what appeared to be the lyrics to 'What Shall We Do With a Drunken Sailor?', but with lots of pursing of the lips and eyebrow raises. Mina couldn't help but be amused.

'Lukie, you're freezing.' She unwrapped her woollen shawl and went to put it round her cousin, which seemed to rouse him from his trance.

'Ugh! Get that fugly thing off me!' Lukie cried, then glanced about. 'Mina, where the hell am I? How did I even get here? I don't even remember going out . . .'

'You were sleepwalking, or rather sleepdancing, again.' Mina looked down at Lukie's feet. 'Somehow you managed to do it all wearing a pair of my shoes.'

He nodded. 'My toes are killing me.'

'Well, maybe take them off for the walk home. And can I see, is that a dress of mine . . .?'

Mina slowly prised the fabric from Lukie's hands. It was indeed an old dress of hers. It appeared to be pinned, as if for adjustment. What on earth was going on?

The following night, Mina woke up to find Lukie attempting to put on her wedding dress. A girl has limits when it comes to Chantilly lace, so she decided that expert help must be called in. Mina went to Dr Seward at the insane asylum, and managed to persuade him that Lukie hadn't ghosted him and was just poorly.

She begged the doctor to recommend a specialist in the kind of symptoms that Lukie displayed, and he gave her the name of one Dr Abraham Van Helsing . . .

•

It was a fresh kind of morning in Amsterdam, and Van Helsing was just returning from a cycle and picking up some discounted vials of botox and fillers. He had a few new clients today, in need of some budget plastic surgery, for which his internet PhD undoubtedly qualified him to just have a go. How hard could it be? It wasn't brain surgery, and no one had died yet, well, so he thought – there had been the sepsis case last week, which hadn't been pretty . . .

Van Helsing shuddered at the thought and fluffed some tulips in a vase to take his mind off such matters. It was then that he saw the telegram on the table.

Dr Van Helsing,
*   Please help. Cousin afflicted by mysterious*
illness. Symptoms include:
- *sleepless nights and sleepwalking/dancing*
- *exhaustion*
- *pale complexion*
- *ruby-red lips*
- *mouthing of lyrics*
- *stealing my clothes*

- *raised eyebrows*
- *hips that mysteriously grow and contract*
Please help! What could it be?
  Mina

'Vell vell vell,' muttered Van Helsing, stroking his chin. Could this be what he thought it was . . .?

He sent an urgent telegram back.

Pix plz

Startled, Mina sent a photo of her cousin.

Van Helsing let out a low whistle when he saw Lukic's visage. 'Damn, bitch.' He sent one more telegram to Mina.

Does the victim also show a fascination with capes?

Back in Whitby, Mina paused and thought. Lukie had always liked a cape, but he just had the one or two, in sensible navy and forest green, and she'd not noticed any untoward interest in them of late. She went to her cousin's bedroom, glancing swiftly at the bed where he lay in a deep slumber. This was all for his own good, wasn't it? Taking a deep breath, she pulled open the doors of the wardrobe, and out tumbled a mass of capes, all black, all with a distinctive red lining! Mina screamed in horror! She sent back a message, immediately.

Yes. YES. There are scores of the devils!

Van Helsing read the message in Amsterdam, and furiously scrunched it up. So, the old bat was making a comeback, with a ripe new talent in her claws. This could not happen!

Back in Whitby, Mina received a simple message:

Urgent case of cape–itis. On my way.

•

Up in the abbey, Dragula was feeling more renewed and vigorous than she had in years. She'd been trying sleeping upside down with a silk eyemask on, and the rush of blood to the head had really plumped out those crow's feet. The girls were proving a lot less trying as well, happily heading off into town to let their hair down each night. But the biggest factor of all was undoubtedly Lukie Westenra's transformation into the brightest new star in the House of Dragula, which was so nearly complete. Dragula had never seen a young queen develop so fast! The journey had given Dragula back her confidence and enthusiasm – yes, bring on the VAMPageant like a sacrificial virgin to the altar.

Dragula peeked out from the eyemask and reached for a packet of Scampi Fries. Nearly sundown, and tonight they'd be helping Lukie get to grips with lip-syncing with the fangs. Dragula tumbled off her perch and began applying a basic face. She could do with running J-Hark's razor over the six o'clock shadow again, but never mind. Talking of Jonathan, Dragula hoped he was alright. He hadn't reappeared again in Whitby yet, although Mina wasn't too bothered by it, according to Lukie.

'Dragula! Dragula, I'm here!' called Lukie, dashing into the abbey.

'Hello, my dear,' called Dragula, and the Daughters emerged blearily from their crates of eyelashes. 'Everyone into heels for practice, and Lukie, perhaps a hoop skirt just so you can get the hang of it.'

Lukie nodded and got changed into one of Mina's cast-off petticoats.

'You look criminal in those crinolines,' purred Fangela, running a finger over Lukie's collarbone.

Young love! thought Dragula fondly, and slightly idealistically. *Nice to see the girls keeping it in the family, even if they can't keep it in their pants.*

The rehearsal began, focusing on one of Dragula's classic showstoppers – 'Like An Undead Virgin' – and all was going well.

But wait, who is this lurking in the shadows, watching the proceedings with a barely concealed fury – and more than a hint of jealous insecurity about the sheer talent that's on display?

Babebraham Van High Heelsing stepped forward into a beam of moonlight, six foot six of dairy-fed Dutch realness, clad head to toe in a black latex catsuit and full hood, only her eyes visible, and a whip-like blonde ponytail sprouting out the top. The girls stopped their lip-syncing and gasped, which caused Dragula to turn round and face her nemesis – so fucking *typical* that Van High Heelsing would appear looking flawless when Dragula was rocking a chin that was fuzzy as a duckling and wearing a jogging pants and espadrilles combo that was truly chilling.

'Vell, vell, vell, the tired old bat is back in action, it would appear,' Van High Heelsing sneered. 'Are times so hard that you're cutting back on everything, apart from that stubble?'

Dragula kept her cool. 'I can't hear a word you're saying through that hood, Babebraham. For which I am eternally grateful.'

Annoyed, Van High Heelsing quickly unzipped the mouth of the hood. 'OK, *ja*, so that's better? *I said*, the tired old bat is back in action, it would appear.'

'This tired old bat is coming for your crown. Or should that be *my* crown, given who won it fair and square,' hissed Dragula, sucking her teeth and regretting it instantly.

Van High Heelsing threw back her head and laughed. 'The only thing that's square around here is your arse. Dragula, you better just ztick to that liquids-only diet and get back to your coffin – your career is dead anyway. But you.' Here she turned to Lukie and walked over slowly, navigating the rough terrain perfectly in stilettos – you have to give the bitch credit where it's due. 'You, my little darling – you belong with a mother who can give you what you deserve – and that's contouring. It's like I say: if you ain't Dutch, you ain't much.'

Quick as a flash, Dragula darted over and zipped up the mouth on Van High Heelsing's hood, snapping off the zip fastening and swallowing it. 'Good luck unpeeling yourself out of that thrush factory, you nasty sweaty *cheat*! And if I see you coming around here after my girls again, I won't hesitate to pop those pneumatic boobies of yours!' The Daughters applauded, and a furious Van High Heelsing hobbled away, muffled expletives issuing from the catsuit.

Despite her sass, Dragula was shaken up. Van High Heelsing had looked at the top of her game. Maybe she *was* just a tired old bat after all. But then she looked round at the shining eyes of Lukie Westenra.

'Dragula, Dragula, can we do . . . cape? I really feel like I'm getting the hang of the swooshing.'

Dragula's creaky old raisin heart blossomed at the sight of such unfettered enthusiasm, undiminished by backstage bitchery or blocked pores. Let Van High Heelsing do her worst! 'Yes, my dear. We can do cape *forever.*'

•

Mina was somewhat bemused by the antics of her Dutch visitor. Dr Van Helsing had arrived in a foul mood, carrying scraps of some shiny black fabric, and had immediately insisted on festooning Lukie's bedroom with charms to drive out the cape-itis – a 'foul and dangerous' disease, if Van Helsing's diagnosis was to be believed. He'd also 'driven out the nest of capes'; rather an over-dramatisation, Mina thought, given that his actions consisted of chucking the capes down the stairs with lots of shrieking and telling her to burn them. Mina didn't quite have the heart to destroy them all, as the needlework on them was lovely, so she kept one in the garden shed instead.

'What is the cure?' asked Mina tentatively, looking at Lukie fast asleep on the sofa.

'The cure is sleep!' snapped Van Helsing. 'Lots of sleep and daytime and boring clothes, we must keep Lukie awake all the day so he will sleep soundly at night.'

Van Helsing insisted on marching Lukie through Whitby in a pair of sturdy brogues until he was dead on his feet. As soon as nightfall came, Van Helsing dosed Lukie with a sleeping draught and tucked him tightly into bed. Checking Mina was nowhere in sight, Van Helsing added a garland of photographs around the window – signed pictures of High Heelsing in her winner's crown, along with a multitude of garlic bulbs with the note 'REMEMBER ME?' tacked to one of them. *That should keep the old bat at bay*, he thought with a smirk.

That night, when Lukie did not appear at the abbey as usual, Dragula popped down to the town with the intention of tapping on his window pane. *Ugh! What horror is this?* Dragula recoiled at the sight of Van High Heelsing's tacky photographs and the stench of garlic, which brought a vivid memory of the exact sensation of stacking it, Naomi Campbell-style, on the runway. Lukie's curtains were open just enough that Dragula could catch a peek of the young protégé, deep in slumber – and watched over by the Dutch she-devil herself.

Van High Heelsing looked up and caught Dragula's eye, smirking and raising a finger to his over-puffed lips.

Dragula was furious. Van High Heelsing was playing on her good manners – she wouldn't *dream* of entering the boudoir without an invitation! – and the reek of garlic was overwhelming and threatening to bring about a full-blown flashback. Dragula darted away, and back to the abbey to formulate another plan. It was essential that Lukie's transformation was completed in time for the return to Transylvania; time was short as it was, without the interference of a cunning Dutch legend – who knew what lies Babebraham was pouring into Lukie's ear as he slept, no doubt trying to convert him into joining the House of Van High Heelsing.

Dragula's suspicions were right. Van High Heelsing crooned the temptations of the Netherlands for hours. 'Ve haff a beautiful canal house, right in the centre of Amsterdam. You will be out every night, enjoying the nightlife, living your dreams, crowds gathered to praise each step you take on the runway! You can go out in daylight and eat *poffertjes* and herring to your heart's content, not be stuck in some stinky cold castle in the middle of nowhere. And, Lukie, I currently haff an offer on facial fillers and botox, if, you know, you want freshening up.' Van High Heelsing couldn't resist putting her fingers either side of Lukie's face and tweaking it up. Too early for a full lift, but a cheeky filler never went amiss. But wait, what was this crinkled under Lukie's pillow? Van High Heelsing pulled out a crumpled piece of paper and smoothed it out, gasping. *The VAMPageant!*

•

After a few days of Van Helsing's treatment, Lukie was improving rapidly. He no longer slept throughout the day, but throughout the night, his colour had returned, and there had been no further midnight attempts on Mina's wardrobe.

'I zink that this should be vun of my success stories,' said Van Helsing, smugly nibbling a breakfast kipper. 'But, cape-itis can return and become chronic. It's probably better if Lukie returns with me to Amsterdam for more extensive treatments.'

'Oh,' said Mina, disappointed. 'Is that really necessary? I was hoping he could stay here, you know, be with his family. He was meant to be helping me with my wedding dress.'

Van Helsing shuddered and slammed his hand down on the table, making the marmalade jump and rattle. '*Nein!* Mina, it is imperative that Lukie is kept away from all tempting fabrics! Indeed, all forms of needlework. It's why he must come to Amsterdam where he will be quarantined in such a way as to ensure his constant safety.'

'Well, surely we can ask Lukie what he wants?' said Mina. She turned to her cousin, who sat staring at the tablecloth and plucking it with his fingers.

'Mina, this cloth must be removed by nightfall,' added Van High Heelsing, with a click of the fingers. Mina was getting heartily sick of his bossiness.

'It's gingham, it's hardly a temptation.'

'To the recovering cape-itis victim, *everything* is a temptation. Why this could be thrown over the shoulder and look, it's a cape, picnic vibes, little Rude Riding Hood, etc.'

At this, Lukie looked up, a glimmer of interest in his eyes. Mina couldn't help but notice that even though her cousin was supposedly getting better, he was a lot less happy than he'd seemed while in the grip of cape-itis fever.

'What do you want, Lukie?' she said, reaching out to touch her cousin's arm.

He shrugged, putting a finger to his teeth. 'I don't know, Mina. I had the most wonderful dreams, and I thought they were real, but now . . . It's all fading.'

'These dreams were but hallucinations, Lukie!' said Van Helsing firmly. 'You must put them out of your mind once and for all.'

'But you feel better, don't you?' said Mina.

Lukie turned to her, his eyes full of sadness. 'I don't know.'

'*Ja*, of course he does!' chimed in Van Helsing. 'It's normal to feel a little tiredness after the exertions of the runway . . . I mean the fever.'

At this, Lukie looked up, eyes narrowed. What did the Dutch doctor mean by that? Lukie couldn't shake off the feeling that he'd seen him somewhere before . . .

•

Things weren't looking good for Dragula's comeback. Lukie's brutal sleep hygiene routine and the noxious presence of the garlic-n-pix wreath made it impossible to get to the young protégé. But then, a bit of luck came Dragula's way.

Stroke of Luck No. 1 came in the form of Mina clearing out Lukie's room, grossed out by the reek of stale garlic and the pictures some tacky harlot had left strewn about. Stroke of Luck No. 2 arrived in the form of Lukie taking some air in the back garden. Trying to come to terms with the fact that Dragula had been a hallucination of a fevered mind, Lukie saw a scrap of fabric peeking out from the shed door. Heart pounding, he darted over and pulled it out – it was a cape! Black, high-collared and lined in red. Lukie clutched it to his heart. No matter what Van Helsing had told him, about his 'hallucinations', Dragula was *real*.

That night, Lukie feigned a deep slumber before Van Helsing could give him his medicine. As soon as the Dutch disaster had left his bedroom, Lukie resolved to stay awake, and lit a candle in his window to encourage Dragula's presence. He was learning fast about flattering lighting.

Shortly after midnight, Lukie heard a tapping on the window pane. He leapt out of bed, pulled back the curtains and saw Dragula peering in.

'Dragula! I thought you were a dream!' cried Lukie, and Dragula gestured frantically for him to be quiet.

'Can I come in, darling?' asked the Count.

'Yes, of course, of course,' replied Lukie, flinging open the window and helping Dragula clamber in – no mean feat with those hips. 'But where have you been? I didn't understand what was happening. Van Helsing told me it was all a dream.'

Dragula's expression darkened. 'Lukie, darling, there are things you must know about Van Helsing, or should I say, Van High Heelsing . . .' Dragula told Lukie of their past, their friendship, the stolen crown and the terrible rift between them.

'I knew it!' said Lukie. 'She mentioned the runway today.'

Dragula nodded. 'And I tried to come here every night, but you were always so sound asleep, and then Babebraham had put garlic and those awful photos all around the window with no trigger warning, and my dear – I couldn't stay long . . . Yet all the time, I suspected she would be singing to you in your sleep, trying to lure you to the house of Van High Heelsing.'

Lukie shook his head. 'I don't remember.'

'May I look under your pillow?'

Lukie nodded, and Dragula went over to the bed and pulled out a latex stocking from underneath the pillowcase.

Lukie gasped in horror, and Dragula nodded grimly. 'I knew it. Trying to infiltrate your dreams with her signature look. Thank God I reached you tonight. But, darling, our time is short if we're to complete your transformation and reach Transylvania in time for the VAMPageant.'

Lukie nodded. 'I'm ready, Dragula. I know I'm ready.'

•

Mina awoke with a jolt. The church bells could be heard ringing in the distance, but it was something different that had woken her from a deep sleep. She thought she'd heard her bedroom door shutting softly and, now she listened further, she was convinced there was an intruder in the house – she could hear quiet footsteps.

Heart pounding, Mina sat up and got out of bed. Softly, she opened the door and crept down the corridor. A light showed dimly under Lukie's bedroom door. Fear prickled down her spine. A sound behind her made her jump; she turned to find Van Helsing emerging from the guest bedroom, with a candle in hand.

'I think there's a burglar,' she whispered as he drew next to her.

'*Ja*, I zink so as well,' he muttered. 'Let's go and see. You first.'

Forcing herself to take courage, Mina tiptoed further down the corridor. She paused only briefly before Lukie's bedroom, to catch up a parasol that she supposed would do as a weapon, and then burst into the room.

What a scene greeted them! Dragula had just finished applying Vampire's Kiss to Lukie, who was seated with his back to the door, and raised the lipstick high in triumph.

'Godverdomme!' gasped Van High Heelsing, behind her. 'Ve are too late! The transformation is complete!'

'What transformation?' cried Mina. 'Lukie's sickness, has it returned?'

'Pffff!' said Dragula, with some fang difficulty. 'She's not sick – she's *sickening*!'

Lukie rose up and twirled around. 'Meet Lucy Wonderbra – serving fresh fish to the people of Whitby!' Lucy was a stone-cold fox and no mistake. She was dressed in Mina's high-necked wedding dress, which had been altered to reveal more thigh than would probably have been originally acceptable in a nineteenth-century parish church and dyed the blackest black. The look was finished with a high-necked, glittering black cape, which Lucy swished round dramatically, and a pair of jet earrings large enough to warrant their own passport.

'Oh, Lukie! I mean, Lucy, you look beautiful!' said Mina. 'And I love your hair! It's just like mine, no?'

Lucy looked awkward, and raised a hand to her crown of auburn tresses. 'Mina, dearest cousin – it *is* yours.'

Mina put a hand up to her hair and realised it had been cropped short.

'It suits you, though!' said Dragula, gesturing extravagantly. 'It's very gamine, very Liza Minnelli in *Cabaret*. And we had to think of something last minute, we tried not to wake you – *someone* has bought up the rest of the wigs in town.' She glared at Van Helsing.

'Well I wish you'd asked,' said Mina crossly. 'And I presume that's my wedding dress?'

Lucy looked abashed. 'Mina, I'm sorry . . . I was just carried away, this all happened so quickly!'

Mina sighed and put a hand to Lucy's cheek. 'I know. And I can see how happy you are, but—'

'But nothing!' shrieked Van Helsing, diving for Lucy Wonderbra. 'You'll come with me, Lukie! This cape-induced madness will stop!'

With a flip of her cape, Dragula deflected Van Helsing like an expert bullfighter, causing the doctor to become momentarily confused. Dragula took the split-second advantage and fled, diving out of the window with Lucy in tow.

'When will I see you again, dear cousin?' called Mina, rushing to the window, but the two figures were fast disappearing up towards the abbey steps.

'What the hell was that about?' she said, turning back to Van Helsing, who was huffing and puffing on the floor.

'Your cousin is in grave danger,' he began.

'Oh *please*,' said Mina angrily. 'The only thing that's been in danger around here is my hair. Lucy's happy! I've never seen her so animated! Just leave them be and sod off back to Amsterdam.'

'Lukie's happy now,' said Van Helsing, drawing on all his cunning. 'But he won't be when he is a prisoner in Dragula's castle, forced to do the same old boring routines, his career over before it's even begun. And hundreds of miles away, surrounded by wolves and the wilderness of Transylvania. You won't ever see him again, dear Mina. You should listen to me, and I will help you win him back . . .'

Mina felt herself waver. Was what Van Helsing said true?

'Sleep on it, pumpkin,' said the Dutch deceiver, and sashayed away.

Mina was in turmoil the following day. She managed to avoid Van Helsing's kipper-breathed enquiries and went to bed early, hoping a plan of action would become clear. Some consolation was provided by her new haircut, however. Dragula had, admittedly, done a great job and it brought out her cheekbones like there was no tomorrow.

Shortly after midnight, there came a tapping on the window. She bounded out of bed and went to peek. *Lukie!*

Elated, Mina flung open the window and embraced her cousin. 'Are you back for good? I was thinking, we could see if there's a slot on at the Olde Seagull, I'm sure you'd go down a treat.'

'Oh, Mina, my dear, it breaks my heart to leave you, but I have my eyes set on bigger runways than walking the plank at the local. I've come to say goodbye,' said Lukie, taking her hands.

'Goodbye?' Mina whispered. 'But . . . but . . .'

Dragula popped up next to Lukie, panting heavily after the climb up to the window. 'Mina, babe, can I borrow some moisturiser?'

Mina nodded, and pointed to her dressing table. Dragula clambered in and began applying the ointment to her knees. 'Darling, I know it's hard for you. But I will take good care of Lucy.'

'Van Helsing said otherwise,' said Mina. 'He said that you'd take Lucy to some horrible castle in the middle of nowhere.'

Dragula stiffened. 'Castle Dragula is due a refurb but the facilities are perfectly adequate . . . Which reminds me, have you seen anything of that dear fiancé of yours?'

Oh him! thought Mina. 'No, I haven't. Why?'

'No reason!' said Dragula, a trifle furtively. 'But, I promise you, this is what Lucy wants. And you'll see each other again soon! Once we get the tour dates sorted.'

Mina looked miserable. 'But I don't want to be left here without my best friend and with only Van Helsing for company. God knows where Jonathan has got to. Can't I come with you?'

She looked imploringly at Dragula.

Lukie clapped his hands. 'Oh, Dragula, please! Please!'

Dragula sighed. 'I'm not sure . . .'

'I won't be any trouble,' said Mina. 'And besides, I can do Lucy's hair! Who knows those tresses better than I?'

She had a point, thought Dragula. The scruffy up-do was passable for a fledgling queen, but soon Lucy would have to bring something more ornate. Plus, it wouldn't really be a drag show without a drunk straight girl shrieking, and Mina would be perfect for that – Dragula could tell she would be a bit of a tinker after a few Bacardi Breezers.

'Fine!' said Dragula. 'My dear, you shall go to the ball! We leave tonight – there is no time to dilly dally!'

•

The next day at dawn, a weary Jonathan Harker collapsed at the front door of the Whitby cottage. It had been a long, long trek back from Transylvania, and he was looking forward to being back in the arms of Mina and forgetting all about the frights of the castle.

He raised an arm to knock at the door, having lost his keys somewhere in the forest trying to extract sap from a tree for sustenance, but the door swung open before his hand could connect, and Jonathan found himself staring at the very pointed toe of a stiletto latex boot.

'Jonathan Harker, I presume,' came a nasally voice from above. 'Vot took you so long? Ve're in the shit.'

A strong hand clutched Jonathan by the scruff of his neck and hauled him over the threshold. *Was this some sort of role play by Mina?* Jonathan wondered briefly, and not without a moment of hope. *She'd been talking about spicing things up, but this was a little too much before the wedding*. He was dumped unceremoniously in an armchair by the fireplace, and the figure sat down in the chair opposite.

Gee Whillickers! thought Jonathan, upon examining his assertive companion, and no wonder. Van High Heelsing had finally taken her medical career seriously, dressing in a latex nurse's outfit which she considered both stylish and practical given the wipe-clean nature of the fabric. She extended one long leg in the air, flexed and extended it.

'You like vot you see, Mr Harker?' she purred.

Jonathan nodded dumbly.

'Vell good, because you're not going to like what I tell you. Dragula has kidnapped Mina and Lukie, and taken them to the castle!'

Jonathan screamed in horror. Mina, suffering the ignominies of a communal bathroom – it didn't bear thinking about!

Van High Heelsing cringed. 'Please stop with zis emotion, it makes me extremely uncomfortable. And it gets worse. Dragula has transformed Lukie into . . . one of her own kind.'

Jonathan gasped. 'We must save them – and who, who are you?'

The Dutch bombshell attempted a smile through the layers of botox and surgical enhancement, the strain of which was practically audible. 'I, my dear, am Dr Van High Heelsing. Bringing a new Dutch Golden Age when I take to the stage. And luckily for you, I am going to save the day – and that annoying little fiancée of yours if I have to. But we have little time, Jonathan. You must wash – please – and pack lightly, and then we must return to Transylvania post-haste to stop Dragula's terrible plans.'

Jonathan's heart sank. He'd just come from that infernal place, after spending days wandering through the forest, quite lost. Couldn't he just . . . stay in Whitby?

As if she'd read his thoughts, Van High Heelsing fixed him with a piercing gaze. '*Nein*, Jonathan!'

PART THREE

The Return to Transylvania

Both our kweens are now on their way,
To the scene of the crime – that fatal runway.
Dragula and co are travelling economy,
But it's fun below stairs, in all honesty.
High Heelsing and Jonathan are going first class,
Via Amsterdam, so Babe can pump up that ass.
Who will triumph, that is the question,
Reader, play on, that's my suggestion.

Lil Bloodsucker was having a sundowner outside the Junk Emporium, contemplating the VAMPageant, which presently had zero entries. She sighed, and wondered whether Mr Cummerbund could be persuaded to frock up, or if she should just sack it all off and accept that the TV scene was well and truly over. She'd hoped the VAMPageant might goad Dragula out of hiding, but she hadn't heard a squeak from the old bat.

She turned and wandered back into the shop, then began to close up with a heavy heart. Then she heard the sound of a throat being cleared behind her. Lil whipped round to see a silhouette in the doorway – a tall, *caped* silhouette, one that made the hairs on the back of her neck stand up.

'What's your returns policy?' said Dragula, drawing on the tail-end of a cigarette, throwing it to the ground and grinding it out with a cork wedge that she'd been persuaded to try instead of the omnipresent espadrille.

Lil's heart was pounding. 'Dragula! You're making a comeback?'

'Well, actually I still need to exchange that corset but – yes. The old bat is coming back. For the VAMPageant, if you'll have me. I promise I'll be good.'

Lil Bloodsucker sprang out from behind the counter and embraced Dragula. 'Oh, but we've missed you! We've missed the shows, the glamour, the *fun!*'

Dragula felt a tear prickle her eye. This would not do. She patted Lil Bloodsucker on the back and focused on doing mindful breathing.

'Vell, the competition will be neck and neck,' a harsh voice uttered, and the two of them jumped round to be faced with the gleaming silhouette of Van High Heelsing in the doorway, polishing the VAMPageant crown. 'I hope you and your new little puppy are not afraid of a little competition, Dragula. I'm here to defend my title. I'm not losing to a buffet-pumped old queen with more back rolls than the Dutch under-21s' gymnastic squad.'

Dragula's eyes glowed red with rage. 'I'm not afraid of a *fair* competition, Van High Heelsing, but if you dare pull one of your tricks again . . .'

'You'll do what, exactly?' said Van High Heelsing, running a finger over a dusty selection of rhinestones. 'Afraid that Lucy will see sense and come running to me?'

Dragula snorted. 'Unlikely, Van High Heelsing.'

Babebraham smirked. 'I'll see you on the runway, dear. And stay away from any garlic, won't you?' She mimed a throw, causing Dragula to flinch and reel backwards. Van High Heelsing giggled and sashayed away.

'Are you alright?' said Lil Bloodsucker, going to mix them both a Bloody Mary. 'Don't fall for her mind games. She's looking good, but she's bound to do the same old shit as always. And she wouldn't be here trying to intimidate you if she didn't think you were serious competition.'

Dragula nodded. 'But Van High Heelsing is not to be underestimated. She has been honing her craft, whereas I've been rather . . . indulging myself recently.' Dragula patted her tum. 'She's as driven as a headless horseman's carriage.' Dragula knocked back her Bloody Mary. 'I need to go and practise, Lil.'

Lil smiled. 'Make it count, Dragula.'

Dragula groaned and waggled a finger at her. 'You've been saving that one, I can tell.'

•

The VAMPageant was set for a week's time, and the village erupted into a frenzy of preparation when it was known that the two deadliest rivals would be back in competition. Drag fans from all over Transylvania and beyond poured in, and the Cummerbunds found themselves fully booked for the first time in years. Van High Heelsing stalked the village daily, bellowing about how she had the tightest tuck in Europe, and ordering Jonathan to hand out flyers.

But while Van High Heelsing's confidence grew, things were not so happy at Castle Dragula. Dragula had the girls rehearsing a classic number from back in the day, which involved much cackling, organ music and sweeping gestures with the cape, plus holding a torch under their faces for the lip-synced sections.

'No! NO!' shrieked Dragula for the billionth time, as Lilith got tangled up in Lucy's cape and Fangela kept holding the torch above her head and not underneath her chin. 'What is wrong with you all? Why can you not understand what I'm asking you to do?'

'We understand, alright, it's just not very good!' shouted Edwina furiously.

'How dare you! This routine is how I made my name! Why, the villagers had never seen anything like it. The fangs, the creepy music, throwing the spiders into the audience – THE CAPE!'

'So then they've seen it before. Why can't we do something new? This is old! OLD, OLD, OLD!'

'It's ICONIC! You are just stubbornly refusing to acknowledge my genius, you have no respect, no talent,

I will tear that cape from you if you're not careful!'

'Oh, let me save you the bother,' sneered Edwina, throwing down the offending garment.

Dragula gasped.

'We could have a different colour, maybe?' said Lucy, attempting to make peace. But this succeeded in infuriating Dragula only further.

'NO! NO NO NO NO NO NO! If I've told you one thing, it is this – we wear black, all black, with the *occasional* red highlight if I see fit, and the signature lip and fangs. What, you would have us cavorting on stage in turquoise and orange? In *feathers*? I thought better of you, Lucy!'

Looking on, Mina recognised a meltdown when she saw one. She caught Dragula's eye and held up a packet of fags. Dragula nodded, and flounced out to the ramparts with her.

'You OK, hun?' said Mina, placing a hand on Dragula's shoulder. They'd grown really rather fond of each other on the journey back to Transylvania.

Dragula sighed, her eyes bright with tears. 'Mina, I don't know if I can do this. The whole "rising from the dead" thing, the House of Dragula's big comeback. The girls hate me.'

'They don't hate you,' said Mina. 'They'd have walked out if they didn't want to be here.'

'Well, it's not quite that easy – I do own their souls for all eternity – but thank you for the words.'

'You just need a quick break, all of you,' said Mina.
'Then you'll go back and nail that routine like the lid
of a coffin!'

Dragula shook her head, exhaling a cloud of smoke
into the cold night air. 'Dear child. But the thing is,
they're right. I know it deep down. This isn't working.
But I don't know if I should stick with who I was, what
I know, or try something new . . .'

Mina nodded. 'It's hard stepping out of your comfort
zone.'

'Yes. It's hard to know if you are being true to yourself,
or thinking of other people and what they will do . . .'

'Are you talking about Van High Heelsing?'

Dragula sighed. 'Yes. I hear she has been working
on some ghastly ping-pong routine she picked up in the
Red Light District.'

Mina shuddered. 'It sounds very unhygienic.'

'But it's novel. It's new. It gives the crowd something
to cheer for.'

'But, Dragula, you don't need to resort to such cheap
tricks. Just be yourself.'

Dragula smiled, a little wistfully. 'Alas, I can't help that.
I can't stop thinking of last time I was on the runway. The
happiest moment of my life, then suddenly the sunlight
and the foul stench of garlic and I was tripping over that
terrible bulb and then . . . Everything was ruined!'

Dragula had the kind of breakdown that makes TV
gold, mascara streaming down her face and an eyelash

crawling free like an errant caterpillar. It may actually be a caterpillar – Dragula is fond of a natural beauty hack when budgets are tight. 'And I'm so scared of it happening again! I just want to pretend it never happened!'

'But, Dragula, it did,' said Mina gently. 'And you must confront this. It's part of what made you.'

A wolf howled 'yassss kweeeeeeen!' in the distance. Dragula turned to Mina, a glint in her eye, and threw the sodden caterpillar away. 'Darling, you are brilliant. I have an idea. Can you help me sew a little something . . .?'

•

The day of the VAMPageant dawned. Dragula and the girls had been working flat out and kept to their coffins until sundown. Van High Heelsing was so confident of victory that she had already forced Jonathan to take some new promotional shots of her wrapped in a winner's sash and little else. Jonathan found them rather lewd in tone, there was a lot of finger licking and snarling, but perhaps this was a Dutch tradition.

'Is today the day we find Mina?' he asked tentatively. Hanging out with this Dutch blond-shell had proved to be rather exhausting, and he had a funny rash that could do with being looked at, plus there'd been no mention at all of rescuing his fiancée from Dragula's clutches for quite a few days.

'What queen is that?' snapped Van High Heelsing. 'Some late-entrant bitch from Germany?'

'No, no! My fiancée! Remember? Dragula took her?'

'Oh, yes. Well, we will save her at the show tonight, she will no doubt be there, forced by Dragula to witness her horrifying performance. Fret not, Jonathan, we will save her. In the meantime, could you just hand out some more of those flyers . . .'

•

That evening the villagers crowded into the town hall, which had been transformed into a glittering cavern of wonder. The hay bales had been moved to the side and the pigs mostly chased out. The stage was draped with red curtains and the runway was lit with hundreds of candles. Lil Bloodsucker stepped on stage, dressed in an enormous emerald-green dress, with fairy wings and a towering Marie Antoinette-style wig.

'Children, hush! And welcome back to TV, the drag scene that refuses to die. We have a legendary showdown tonight between two queens with rather a lot of history between them . . . Van High Heelsing, reigning VAMP, and Dragula, ready to bite back!' The crowd whooped – and some booed, too. Backstage, Dragula swallowed nervously. She couldn't rely on the crowd's unconditional support any more. Some would doubtless be glad to see her vanquished forever.

'I'll remind you of the rules,' continued Lil Bloodsucker. 'The only biting we want to see is biting *wit*. And that's pretty much it! We have three categories tonight. The first is "The Legend Lives On", in which queens will showcase the very essence of their drag. Then it's back to the library for a little light reading, before we move into the drag-mother of all lip-syncing for the finale!'

In the crowd, Mina tried to quell her nerves. She was standing with some legendary queens who had returned to see Dragula's comeback – Nosferatutu, Hairy Shelley, who'd darted in at the last minute with her sideburns on fleek, and the Sisters Grimm, who insisted on speaking in perfect unison and weren't very good at making eye contact with anyone apart from each other.

Lil gestured for a moment's calm.

'First to the runway, I call Van! High! Heelsing!'

Mina swallowed. This was it. What had the doctor prescribed?

She was dumbfounded when a lilting accordion tune started up – folk music?! Van High Heelsing emerged on the runway wearing Dutch costume and the crowd murmured in shock and disappointment.

'What the folk is that?' said Lil Bloodsucker, accidentally-on-purpose into the mic.

Babebraham wore a white lace cap, her blonde hair styled into two plaits, a shapeless, full-length, dark blue dress, and an apron embroidered with tulips. Things only got worse when Van High Heelsing demurely raised her gown to show the tips of a pair of wooden yellow clogs.

'Dragula, she's lost it!' whispered Lucy, peering out from backstage. 'It's not Frumpy Friday last time I checked!'

Dragula shook her head grimly. 'No, Lucy. Watch on. Do not underestimate her.'

And with that, in one fell swoop, the traditional Dutch music changed to a pounding techno beat, reverberating up through the village hall and sending dust scattering from the rafters. Van High Heelsing whipped off her lace bonnet to replace it with a black latex cap, before tearing off her dress to reveal a gleaming black bodysuit with an eye-poppingly teeny corseted waist, risqué cut-outs and more bells and whistles than a nineteenth-century policeman. She jumped free of the clogs – double shoe reveal, why not? – and the crowd went nuts for her thigh-high, tightly laced boots with a vicious stiletto heel. A riding crop was tossed to Van High Heelsing from backstage, which she caught and then flexed between her teeth, before smacking it on her boots with a sharp crack as she began to sashay down that runway with a high-stepping walk and a swerve of the hips that could have slayed millions. The crowd went wild, especially when Van High Heelsing lightly spanked Mrs Cummerbund on the way down. Reaching the end of the runway, she leapt into the air and down into a death drop.

'Oh she's Scandi-Scandal-ICIOUS!' called Lil, with a regard for geography as scant as Van High Heelsing's outfit.

'Shit,' muttered Dragula, as Van High Heelsing left the stage to howls of approval. She'd never been one to compete in terms of body, it wasn't her thing anyway, but there was no doubt that a drag-starved crowd appreciated an arse that resembled two eggs in a latex hanky. What the hell was she doing, trying something new? That was classic Van High Heelsing and they'd bloody lapped it up.

Out in the crowd, Mina's heart sank. There was no doubt that Van High Heelsing had killed it out there, and the crowd were wild for more. This was Dragula's big moment and the expectations could not be higher.

'She slayed that one like the woodcutter vs the wolf,' Nosferatutu was saying to the Sisters Grimm. 'You can't argue with that.'

They nodded in unison. 'Yes, Dragula needs to pull something special out of the bag. Fairytale endings don't come easily.'

Suddenly, the candles were snuffed out as if by magic, and the crowd was plunged into darkness. Shrieks went up. Then, a single bright moonbeam hit the stage, throwing a silvery spotlight.

'Once upon a time, a magical bulb was planted,' came Dragula's voice, booming throughout the room, causing a young girl near to Mina to squeak, 'It's Dragula, bitch!'

The voice continued: 'In the darkness of the forests of Transylvania, away from the noise and the crowds, the bulb grew. Away from the spotlight, the bulb gathered strength. Ready . . . to *bloom . . . once . . . more*!'

There was a hiss of smoke and the crowd gasped as, spiralling up from the stage floor came what looked like . . . *a huge bulb of garlic*! It was shimmering white in the moonlight, but I mean – wtf, it was a massive clove of garlic on stage. Then, the bulb's stem began slowly to unwind – aha, the stem was composed of two arms, raised overhead and twined around each other, and then the crowd realised –

'It's Dragula! It's a new look! It's a new silhouette! And – she's wearing *white*!' breathed the young girl next to Mina, clutching her arm. Mina could only nod and look on, speechless with wonder and emotion. The costume was more incredible on the runway than she could ever have imagined.

Dragula's dress was long-sleeved and high-necked, the bodice and arms worked in white shining sequins. The skirt flared out, composed of billowing tulle tiers to give the distinctive bulbed shape, and narrowing just above Dragula's feet, which gave the impression that the bulb was levitating off the floor. Dragula's hair was a v. fashion-forward pale grey, twisted and styled in a towering up-do that resembled the very top stem of the garlic bulb.

Dragula worked the crowd. With her back still turned to them, she waved her arms, undulating them slowly, building up the applause until it reached fever pitch. Then, finally, she slowly spun round and turned her face into the full beam of the moonlight. Goosebumps tingled down Mina's spine. Dragula looked incredible. Her face was still deathly white but those mighty brows had been coated in silver glitter, and her eyes picked out in an undeniably modern geometric liner in black, set off by soft pink and green eyeshadow and at least two pairs of hairy caterpillar eyelashes. The signature lip had been traded for a frosted pink, at least for now, and Mina's heart leapt with pride. Those hours she'd spent in the drawing room with the watercolours had finally been put to good use!

'Hello,' said Dragula coyly, waving at the crowd, fingers topped with long spiralling silver nails. The cheers were deafening. 'I hear that you like . . . garlic?'

The crowd howled, and some even began to throw their cloves at the stage, one of which Dragula caught deftly, bared her fangs and bit into, before throwing it back. Some things would never – and should never – change.

'Well, my dears, prepare to meet . . . some unholy aioli.'

Dragula's daughters flounced onto the stage. Fangela, Lilith and Edwina were dressed in green sequinned catsuits, and had enormous backcombed hair crowned with a cluster of white flowers, to resemble wild garlic. Striding forward, they nailed a vogueing routine that had the villagers begging for mercy in the best possible way.

Then Lucy stepped out on stage. Her outfit was themed in a delicate purple, inspired by the colour of a clove of garlic, and matched by a frisky feather boa. Her hair was also a soft purple, rolled back into gentle waves that hung down her back. Lucy wiggled and shimmied across the stage, before coyly peeling away the layers of her dress to reveal a pin-up-style bodice in purple sequins.

'I am delighted to introduce my very newest daughter!' called Dragula, beaming with a pride that shone as brightly as her diamante earrings. 'Please meet . . . Lucy Wonderbra!'

Lucy put her arms behind her head and jutted out her hips.

'Baby girl, aren't you forgetting something?' called Dragula.

Lucy bared a tube of Vampire's Kiss and applied it to her lips, before snarling to reveal her newly minted fangs. Mina screamed until she was hoarse – Lucy had nailed it!

The Daughters stalked down the catwalk, before twirling round and returning to the main stage. Dragula began to walk slowly forward, a queen returning in triumph and soaking up every last moment of it. It was no mean feat getting used to the amount of material billowing around her legs, but it had been worth it. The new silhouette had gone down a storm. A disaster had been turned into a triumph. She reached the end of the runway and stood, arms raised – 'Thank you, my dears, thank you, thank you!' Dragula called, blowing kisses and chomping into bulbs of garlic left, right and centre. God it *was* delicious. Almost enough to make her return to solid foods. Eventually, she turned and sashayed back down the runway, the Daughters following, before turning round and giving them one last twirl of the bulb dress.

Lil Bloodsucker stepped forward. 'Phewee, now that's what I call a couple of comebacks! There'll be a brief interval for mead, then it's time for a little reading with drag mother . . .

'Dragula, it's time for you to step out of the shadows – and into the shade,' said Lil, beckoning Dragula forward and handing her a pair of horn-rimmed glasses. 'The library is open.'

'And I hope you're ready for some classics,' purred Dragula, stepping forward and perching her glasses on her nose. The crowd howled in anticipation. Dragula's tongue was known to be sharper than her fangs.

'My Dutch disaster, it's been a while.' Dragula blew Babebraham a kiss, before turning to the crowd. 'Someone told Van High Heelsing to let her talent shine – my dear, they didn't mean go without powder, you're wetter than an otter's pocket right now!' She offered Van High Heelsing a hankerchief before continuing.

'Van High Heelsing is always talking about how she can make you beautiful with one of her surgical procedures. Well, darlings, Dragula can offer you the original nip' – she pointed to her fangs – 'and tuck!' She thrusted vigorously and Mina collapsed with laughter, along with the rest of the crowd. Van High Heelsing scowled, but Dragula was just warming up and threw zinger after zinger at her arch rival.

'We need to evacuate – there's been a chemical spill – oh wait, it's just Van High Heelsing sweating.'

'Someone call 999 – the good doctor's hair is dangerously dehydrated.'

'I'm glad to see that Van High Heelsing can crack a whip, as she sure can't crack a smile.' Dragula gave a dastardly imitation of Van High Heelsing's paralysed face.

'Van High Heelsing, when was that catsuit last washed? I wouldn't want to go anywhere near *those* Netherlands.' Dragula pinched her nose and gestured towards the crotch of Van High Heelsing's catsuit. Van High Heelsing shifted nervously, causing the catsuit to squeak with perfect comic timing.

The crowd broke into rapturous applause as Dragula handed the glasses to Lil Bloodsucker, who took them and passed them to Van High Heelsing. The Dutch queen put them on, pushing them firmly up her sweaty nose.

'*Zo Dragula*, great work. *Fangs* for all you do for the community.' There was a silence.

Van High Heelsing nervously looked at the crowd, before clearing her throat and continuing with another clanger of a read. 'You may have heard, Dragula isn't CAPEable of upholding the VAMPageant crown!' In the crowd, Mina glanced around, hearing only one or two quiet laughs. The Sisters Grimm were shaking their heads, and Nosferatutu had gone to the bar to get a straw – those teeth really did make drinking impossible, judging by the stains down the front of that leotard.

Dragula put her hand up. 'Please, miss, I don't see a cape anywhere – do you all?' She gestured to the bulb-shaped dress, causing wolf-whistles and applause to break out. 'But I think perhaps we could have a *whip* round to buy Van High Heelsing something new.'

'Shut up!' barked Van High Heelsing as laughter rippled through the room. Dragula held up her hands and allowed the reading to continue.

Van High Heelsing – 'Your eyebrow hair is zo thick, they should use it to fence off buildings.'

'If it keeps you out, I'm fine with that,' sassed back Dragula.

Van High Heelsing flushed beneath her make-up. 'Umm . . . umm . . .'

'Need a little extra time to get those two brain cells rubbing together?'

'What dating website does Dragula use?' said Van High Heelsing triumphantly. 'Neck-romancer.com!'

Finally, a hit. The crowd laughed, but Dragula stole the applause by moving forward and calling, 'Just be careful if anyone tries to give you a love bite!'

There was no doubt that Dragula had slayed the read, but the lip sync was yet to come. By now, the night was in full swing and the crowd were lairy. Both queens had been known back in the day for their phenomenal lip-syncing skills – this one would be hard to call.

Lil Bloodsucker called both queens before her on stage. 'My dear ghouls, you have been asked to prepare a lip sync to "On the Edge of Gory" but . . . I've changed my mind.' A murmur ran through the crowd. What was going on? 'You will be performing a song you both know very well. "Don't Go Staking My Heart".'

Dragula put a hand to her mouth in shock, and the crowd gasped, too. This was a ballsy move by Lil Bloodsucker. 'Don't Go Staking My Heart' had been a legendary performance between Dragula and Van High Heelsing, which they'd then released as a single which had charted at No. 17 in some districts of Romania, and No. 252 in France. Dragula couldn't help but smile at the memories. She and Babebraham had had some wild times promoting that little number. She glanced across at her deadly rival. Natch, she'd slay the hell out of High Heelsing and take that crown, but then maybe they could patch things up. Maybe. But now wasn't the time to think of stretching out a withered claw of friendship. It was time to focus on clawing back that crown.

Back on the dancefloor, someone bumped into Mina. She turned round, ready to have a proper go, only to realise it was *Jonathan*!

'My darling! Your hair!' He touched her cropped tresses.

'Yes, it's something a little different,' replied Mina, waiting for Jonathan's disapproval.

'I love it,' he said, running his fingers seductively along her cheekbones. 'It brings out those killer eyes of yours.'

This was a whole new Jonathan! thought Mina excitedly. 'Who are you cheering for?'

'Well Van High Heelsing brought me here to rescue you from Dragula's clutches, so it's meant to be her, but after that bulb dress – I mean, it has to be Dragula! Would you believe, I didn't have a clue what was going on when I first went to her castle . . . What a Lily Vanilli I was! At least Van High Heelsing opened my eyes in that respect, but my goodness she's a *pain . . .*'

Further conversation was prevented by the opening bars of 'Don't Go Staking My Heart' ringing out. Mina grasped Jonathan's hand tightly as both queens stepped forward.

Dragula tackled the first verse with aplomb, head thrown back, fangs gleaming in the candlelight, which only served to highlight her perfect timing.

Don't go staking my heart,
You couldn't if you tried,
Oh honey, you're such a hot mess
Your face looks like it's been fried!

Van High Heelsing stalked forward and turned it out, her puffed-up pout coated in neon pink and looking flawless.

Don't go staking your heart?
It'd be kindest, you see,
Cos you been serving the same look
For the past cen-tur-eee!

Dragula rolled her eyes and marched across the stage, sweeping an arm out to the crowd and accompanying the next verse with some pretty lolz gestures.

Don't try staking my heart,
I'll snap your neck like a twig,
Dragula's risen, back on top –
Might wanna check your wig!

Van High Heelsing played a blinder at this point, whipping off her wig and throwing it into the crowd to reveal a peroxide crop – even Mina found herself applauding.

Don't go staking your heart?
Babe that's the least of your worries
You might wanna check up on
Those short and curlies!

Van High Heelsing lunged for Dragula's face, grabbing her chin tightly.

'Hold up, bitch,' growled Hairy Shelley. 'This isn't part of the game!'

'She's trying to make Dragula lose her cool,' lisped Nosferatutu, glancing anxiously at Mina.

This wasn't part of the game. Dragula's eyes blazed with fury, and Lil Bloodsucker hastily cued the chorus to avoid things getting physical.

Ooohooo! Everyone knows it! (The two rivals
warbled together.)
You stole my crown (Dragula)
I hate your gown (Van High Heelsing)
Right from the start,
I gave you my art! (Dragula)
I gave you an arse! (Van High Heelsing)

Dragula grudgingly acknowledged that one. Van High Heelsing knew how to pad, plus there'd been the offers of an implant. But fuck it, she'd given Van High Heelsing *hours* of her time, her ideas, her routines, her songs! Dragula moved forward to tackle her verse like a lioness felling a bison.

Don't go staking my heart!
Haven't you heard it said?
Dragula is putting the living
Back into the living dead!

'YES QUEEN!' screamed Mina, leaping up and down. The crowd went wild for that one. Dragula was indeed living, she was strutting her stuff all around the stage, pointing those long nails every which way, then she leapt up, spun around and down into a death drop.

•

Van High Heelsing sensed the mood changing. This called for urgent measures. She flipped backwards and straight down into the splits:

Don't go staking your heart?
Bitch please, suck on this,
The only place you're legendary,
Is in the ce-me-te-reee!

The chorus kicked in again:

Ooohooo! Everyone knows it!
You stole my crown (Dragula)
I hate your gown (Van High Heelsing)
Right from the start,
I gave you my art!
I gave you an arse!

It was time to put this one to bed, decided Dragula. She hadn't tried this little trick in a while, but there was no time like the present. Dragula stepped forward, gesturing to Lucy to chuck her a cape from backstage.

She caught it, and opened it up, swirling it round in a blur of black and sparkle, the crowd screaming, before flinging it round her shoulders and popping up the high collar like the bad bad bitch she was. God, it felt good to be back. Dragula gathered a deep breath.

> Don't go staking my heart!
> There's one way to settle this,
> While you look tragic, I serve magic,
> Sealed with a vampire's kiss!

Dragula began to blow kisses to the crowd – each one of which turned into a tiny silver bat, which fluttered in a swarm above the audience before exploding in glitter that rained down onto the delighted peasants below.

'Maybe you could throw out some Babybels or something, bitch?' breathed Dragula, as she passed by Van High Heelsing. Yeah, she wasn't beyond a bit of cattery when it was called for, and it was a pleasure to shut up that laughing cow.

The roar of the crowd drowned out the backing track, and Lil Bloodsucker emerged on stage, gesturing for a moment's calm.

'My fierce queens, you have both restored honour to the village and the reputation of Transylvania by your performances in this pageant. Dragula, your conduct has been exemplary – I hearby renounce the curse and you will be able to gaze upon that fine visage in the mirror once again!'

Dragula bared her fangs and beamed in relief. It had been a real exercise in trust to let Mina do her make-up – she couldn't wait to get backstage and actually *see* in the mirror how she looked. And who knew, maybe now she could work on a little bit of contouring? Just a little . . . Lil Bloodsucker was continuing.

'And I hope that the two of you can put your history behind you, and make amends.'

Dragula gazed over to her former friend. She was willing to forgive and forget. Eternity was too long to hold a grudge. She extended a hand to Van High Heelsing, who turned to her and smiled – or grimaced, it was hard to tell.

'And now, to announce the winner of the VAMPageant.'

Lil Bloodsucker paused theatrically and the room fell completely silent. Mina crossed her fingers.

'This queen goes straight for the jugular – and straight into our hearts. Dragula, you are the winner of the VAMPageant!'

The crowd roared their approval, Dragula dropped her head into her hands. It had been a long time getting to this moment, facing her fears and daring to try something different while staying true to herself. The haters had said the House of Dragula was over – well, they could go and fuck themselves. Dragula turned round to face her daughters, each one of them clapping wildly. 'Thank you, girls,' Dragula breathed. The little bitches weren't so bad after all.

Dragula stepped forward to stand by Lil Bloodsucker, who held the glittering VAMPageant crown. Lil smiled at Dragula, and raised the crown, ready to lower it onto Dragula's head.

'No!' came a screech. 'The crown is MINE I tell you, mine, mine, mine!' Van High Heelsing hurled herself from across the stage, pushing the Daughters and Lil aside, and grabbed Dragula by the throat, forcing her down. She whipped off one of her stilettos, held it by the toe and raised the sharp heel overhead, ready to strike!

'A heel through the heart, well this should be an interesting follow-up single!' shrieked Van High Heelsing, to gasps of horror.

Just as she began to bring the heel down with all her considerable force, a blurred figure bowled across stage, throwing itself in front of Dragula – and taking the full impact of the stiletto heel.

'Jonathan!' gasped Mina, pushing her way to the front of the crowd and up on stage, where a wriggling Van High Heelsing was being subdued by Lil Bloodsucker, who was a dab hand with a pitchfork.

Jonathan lay on stage, panting for breath, a sheen of sweat gathering on his pale brow. Dragula gathered him in her arms, and Mina arrived by their side.

'Jonathan, Jonathan!' said Mina. 'Are you alright? Are you terribly badly injured?'

Jonathan lifted his eyes to her. 'Mina, my beautiful

Mina . . . I think it might be fatal . . . Van High Heelsing staked my heart with the stiletto!'

Dragula moaned. 'My dear Jonathan, this cannot be, let me see . . . there must be some remedy we can try, we can perhaps stuff the wound with garlic until help arrives, and then if the worst comes to it at least you'll taste delicious . . .' Dragula parted Jonathan's shirt. 'There is no blood! But how?' Then, she felt an object in Jonathan's coat pocket, and pulled it out. It was a familiar-looking gold lipstick tube, now deeply dented where Van High Heelsing's blow had glanced off it.

'I told you this was a miracle formula, girls!' called Dragula.

'Why do you have a thing like that . . .?' said Mina curiously.

'From the night when . . .'

'The girls' little makeover attempt?' said Dragula quickly, before Jonathan could complete his sentence with something like, '. . . you tried to kill me.' That was all history now. 'Yes, I thought I'd lost a lipstick then! But how can I ever repay you? You *saved* me, Jonathan.'

Jonathan glanced at Mina, then leant forward to whisper in Dragula's ear . . .

•

The crowning ceremony was rescheduled for an hour or so later, and the Cummerbunds declared free shots for all in the meantime. Dragula returned to the stage, this time dressed in a silver crushed-velvet gown with enormous puff sleeves, a corseted waist and a full skirt. Her hair was returned to black, with a silver streak running throughout, and the look was completed with a long black cape and scarlet lips plus the finest cubic ziroconia earrings QVC could provide. Lil Bloodsucker called Dragula forward and crowned her as the winning VAMP, embracing her dear pal as the applause rained down. Van High Heelsing grimaced from a pair of fluffy handcuffs at the side of the stage, before Lil sentenced her to community service.

'Van High Heelsing, you are henceforth banished to the Sue Spyder charity shops on the outskirts of Amsterdam, where you will graciously sort and fold all the comfortable cotton underwear!'

The punishment combined two of Van High Heelsing's greatest hates: altruism and natural fibres. She howled furiously as she was led away.

Then Dragula stepped forward, gesturing for a little quiet. 'As you all know, I was nearly vanquished on the runway tonight – and in a rather more literal sense than we're used to. I owe one brave individual a debt of thanks.' Here she paused. 'And I am delighted to be able to repay just some of that debt to *her*. Darling, come forth!'

Wobbling like Bambi on ice, Jonathan Harker emerged in the classic House of Dragula look – the caped silhouette, the red lip, and Fangela had indeed managed to work in the odd stripe or two.

'I am delighted to present . . . Venetia Stiletto! Or should that be, Stilet-NO!' called Dragula, beckoning Venetia to her, taking her hand and raising it aloft. This caused Venetia to wobble precariously, and Lucy darted in to support her from the other side. Venetia strutted, or rather clomped, down the runway, to rapturous cries. She was the heroine of the hour!

The sisters dragged Venetia through most of a dance routine to 'Oops I Bit Again', before leaving the stage. Mina dashed backstage. She hadn't felt this passionate about Jonathan since their first quadrille together!

'Venetia! You were wonderful!' said Mina, hugging Jonathan, who was pulling off his wig and de-cinching rapidly in a bid to catch his breath.

'Thank you, my dearest Mina,' panted Jonathan.

'And leave those heels on,' Mina whispered throatily, drawing him in for a passionate, lipstick-smeared kiss.

. . . *And now we must leave our merry queens,*
(it costs extra to go behind the scenes)
Lucy at home with her drag sisters,
Nursing some well-earned blisters,
Jonathan and Mina happily reunited,
A bit of kink making them delighted.
Van High Heelsing vanquished once more,
To plot a comeback, we can't be sure.
And Dragula, a living dead legend rightly
  crowned,
For world-wide fame surely bound.
Good reader I must bid you adieu,
Until I see you on our global tour.

Ma'am Stoker xxxx